Lily

TRANSPLANTED

THE FLOWER LADIES TRILOGY 2

Lily TRANSPLANTED

D. A. SPRUZEN

Lily Transplanted
Copyright © 2026 D. A. Spruzen. All rights reserved.

4 Horsemen
Publications, Inc.

Published By: 4 Horsemen Publications, Inc.

4 Horsemen Publications, Inc.
PO Box 419
Sylva, NC 28779
4horsemenpublications.com
info@4horsemenpublications.com

Cover Illustration by CD Corrigan
Typesetting by Autumn Skye
Edited by Kris Cotter

Library of Congress Control Number: 2025948198

Paperback ISBN-13: 979-8-8232-1021-8
Hardcover ISBN-13: 979-8-8232-1022-5
Ebook ISBN-13: 979-8-8232-1023-2

Contents

1

The gray hooded figure stood backlit by the city's glow, filtered through sheeting rain. Hilda felt on edge, as if her childhood nightmares were again coming to call.

"Mrs. Wilson? Is this the right house? I couldn't see the number in the dark," a woman said in a gentle voice.

"I am Mrs. Wilson," Hilda said, uneasy still, in spite of the woman's pleasant tone.

"I've come in response to your advertisement for a room to let. Is it still available?"

"Why yes." Hilda nodded, eager now. "Would you like to see it? I'm sorry there's no porch light. I can't climb up on things anymore. My son, so busy you know, hasn't had time to come and change the bulb."

"That's quite all right. Yes, please. I would like to see it."

"Do come in, please. Let me take that raincoat." Looking at the woman in better light and without the dripping coat,

Hilda saw she was quite ordinary, quite lacking the requisites of a nightmare. Medium height, very short dark hair—almost black—and rail thin.

"Please don't trouble yourself. I'm afraid I'm spoiling your beautiful floor."

"No trouble," Hilda answered. "Wait for just a moment while I hang this in the kitchen."

"Most kind."

What formal speech. A good sign, perhaps. Nice manners, too. For Hilda, nice manners stood at the cornerstone of appropriately distant and successful communication with all those who crossed her path, save Magaly. A little give and take could be allowed in that quarter after all these years, her sons, too, but not her daughter-in-law, who was inclined to impertinence given half the chance.

"Come on upstairs," Hilda said. She led the way—a slow climb with Hilda relying heavily on her cane on one side and the railing on the other—and showed her into the room next to the hall bathroom. She loved this little slice of 1940s England with its chintz curtains, matching spread, and rose-strewn carpet. A white chest of drawers straddled one corner and a white armoire presided over a brass bed. The pink silk lampshade cast a warm glow over the room, an inviting room that promised respite. The silk lampshade had been an extravagance, but it had given the room a touch of class, Hilda felt, and she was proud of it.

"Very nice. What are your terms?" The woman kept her face composed. She gave nothing away.

"Well, the advert mentioned the price, $150 a week, payable on Mondays, in advance. That includes fresh sheets and towels once a week and a cooked breakfast every morning. If you want to cook, you'll have to clear it with me in case I have something on. I can give you a shelf in the fridge.

Phew, sorry, I'm a little short of breath!" Hilda paused and panted. The woman's face still told her nothing. "If you make a long-distance call, you must tell me so I can charge you when the bill comes in. You can use the phone for local calls, but not too many calls and nothing very long, mind, and nothing late at night. I have my own bathroom, so the one next door is for your use only."

"That will be quite satisfactory, I know no one here in Toronto," answered the woman, her formality impressing Hilda even more. She looked into Hilda's eyes and her intense gaze was somehow unbalancing, almost indecent. *As if she's looking right through me at someone else*, Hilda thought, again uncomfortable. This woman seemed out of place. Obviously a lady, judging by her demeanor, and well-dressed. Those clothes weren't cheap. What was she doing renting a room in a modest house like this? But Hilda needed the money, and she had no good reason to turn the woman away.

"When would you like to move in?" Hilda asked.

"Oh, right away," she answered. "I don't have much luggage, just one case."

"Lovely, let's go downstairs and have a nice cup of tea," Hilda suggested.

"Thank you," the stranger said as she turned on her heel and disappeared from the room, leaving Hilda to scuttle behind her rigid back as it descended the stairs.

"I expect you can tell from my accent I was born and brought up in England," Hilda said as she bustled around the kitchen. "What about you?"

"I was born in New York, but my family traveled around a lot. I married a Canadian and ended up on a farm in Manitoba. My husband died a few months ago. We had no children." The woman looked down at her clasped hands and seemed to be thinking. "I was never happy in Manitoba, and with our house being so isolated, I couldn't make friends, so I decided to sell everything and try Toronto. I've been staying in a small hotel downtown. I'd rather be in a home." Her arms closed around her waist, as if holding herself in.

"Well, you've had a hard time of it, dear. What's your name?"

"Lily Porter. How do you do?"

"Pleased to meet you, I'm sure. I'd be pleased to offer you the room, Mrs. Porter."

"Call me Lily, please. I'd like to move in tomorrow if that's all right. Would noon suit you?" Lily pulled a wallet out of her bag. "Here's the first week's rent plus another $25 for the extra day since tomorrow's Sunday."

"That suits me very well!" Hilda answered, relieved. She'd cook a nice steak dinner for her and Magaly next week.

"Excellent. I'll see you tomorrow, then." The woman rose before she had finished her tea and strode out. Hilda bustled after her as best she could, not knowing what to make of her new lodger (or "paying guest," as she preferred to say).

As soon as Lily left, Hilda called her friend Magaly, who lived across the street.

"I've got a lodger!" she said, forgetting herself.

"Already? You are a lucky one!"

"Yes, she's a lady, too. Born in New York, married a man from Manitoba, he died a few months ago, so she sold everything off and came to Toronto. What do you think of that? And she paid me the first week in advance! She's moving in tomorrow at noon or thereabouts. Why don't you come in for coffee around that time so you can meet her?"

"I would not miss it for anything."

Magaly was always curious about anything new, as was Hilda. Their world was so small—bordered as it was by tight finances, arthritic old age, and narrowed intellect—that any distraction from daily tedium fostered endless debate and speculation. New situations aroused tense discomfort, automatic disapproval, shifty pondering, sometimes followed by grudging acceptance, and were, indeed, the only excitement they could expect.

Magaly arrived fifteen minutes before noon and arranged herself across her usual chair in Hilda's kitchen. Hilda smiled at her friend with affection that had grown with a reassuring steadiness over the years—they had taken their time getting close to one another. Hilda didn't believe in rushing into things, and she appreciated that Magaly had sensed that she would feel threatened by any hasty assumption of intimacy.

Magaly was a stout Hungarian woman—a peasant, Hilda suspected. She and her husband Bela had escaped from their overrun homeland in 1956 and ended up in Toronto, where Bela had found work in a big restaurant. He was a clever fellow, and they had managed to open their own small lunch café where a loyal group of factory workers ate every day. Bela had always been a good cook and was creative in his preparation of filling and tasty dishes for reasonable prices, including some of his native fare. His acquisition of good cheap produce was also creative and his low overhead could not have been sustained if anyone had thought to ask the right questions. Stuffed cabbage owed its frequent appearance on the menu to Bela's friendship with a produce wholesaler's truck driver. Cabbages were cheap, but free (except for a few complimentary dinners) was better. Goulash made with veal rather than beef was produced with a flourish when his local butcher made a sale off the books—tax evasion being a matter of principle rather than meaningful savings. After a few years, he started to open the café for dinner, and it became a fashionable ethnic hangout for the young professional crowd.

Bela and Magaly had bought their house cheaply because a lonely old woman had never done anything to maintain it from the time she moved in until the day she died in the back bedroom. She had remained in her bed unmissed and unmourned until the neighborhood could no longer ignore her as they had while she lived.

They worked hard to restore the tall old wreck, Magaly scraping and painting as she reared their three children, and Bela hammering and sawing on his one day of rest. At the age of sixty-two, his children grown and gone, and his little café now a thriving restaurant, Bela's heart had given up its nagging to be taken seriously and made a final and fatal protest. He left good insurance, a paid-up, handsome house, and some savings, for which Magaly was grateful. She lived frugally and rarely dipped into her savings, in spite of her middle son's pleas for startup money for his various entrepreneurial schemes. Mikey had never got on in the world, for which he blamed his mother for her lack of vision in refusing to back him. She knew her son a lot better than he knew himself. He was not a businessman and never would be. He was too undisciplined to work successfully for anyone else, and too lazy to stick to anything. (*Nothing like his father*, reflected Hilda, *rather more like a good-looking lodger they'd had once in the lean early years.*) He was a nice boy, but of weak character and Magaly knew she loved him much more than he loved her.

Hilda had learned all this about Magaly in small doses of confidences ingested with almost daily cups of coffee over the course of thirty years. She had shown some of herself, too, but not everything, as she considered that Magaly, while a close friend, was not from a sufficiently refined background to appreciate the subtleties of Hilda's true character.

"Well, Hilda, where is this lady? It has gone noon fifteen minutes back. Late already, not a good sign, I think," said Magaly with a triumphant premonition of doomed enterprise.

"Oh, she's too much of a lady to let me down," Hilda said, rising to the bait as always with tight lips and tighter voice.

The bell rang, and Hilda went to answer the door as fast as infirmities and dignity would allow.

"So sorry to be late," Lily said. "I couldn't get a taxi for ages."

"That's quite all right Mrs. Porter," Hilda said. "I hadn't even noticed the time. Come into the kitchen for a moment and meet my friend from across the street, Magaly."

"Welcome, welcome, Mrs. Porter. I know you will be happy here in Hilda's lovely home. I come for coffee nearly every day and I shall like getting to know you."

"Please, call me Lily, both of you. I'm sure we shall get along very well. Do you mind if I go upstairs and freshen up?"

"Yes, of course. Why don't you take your things up to your room now? I've laid out your towels. When you're ready, come down to the kitchen and have a cuppa with me and Magaly. And you may call me Hilda."

Lily unpacked her things—not many clothes, a small vase, some romance paperbacks, a composition book, and a packet of pencils—and put them away in the chest of drawers and armoire. She used to need a large walk-in closet for her clothes and another in the spare room for out-of-season outfits, and here she was, not even filling the small storage space in her new haven. She should consider this meager ownership another kind of freedom, although she'd like some new clothes. It was still warm in early September, but she'd soon need some warm winter separates and an overcoat, too—she'd discarded her last one. It had been bright red with black trim and bold, brassy buttons, good quality, and an irresistible price in that upscale Syracuse thrift shop. She'd looked good in it, but was the sort of coat that made people notice her. A stupid mistake, and she couldn't afford any more of those. She set out her toiletries on a shelf in the bathroom, then tiptoed down the stairs. She paused for a moment halfway down to listen to the conversation in the kitchen.

"Well, Hilda, you have found a nice one, I think. She seems sad. She has not had a good life, I think."

"You may be right, Magaly, but we'll see if we can bring her out a little. And don't forget she is recently widowed, so I'm sure she is still grieving. Perhaps she'll be happy here," Hilda said.

"Yes, well, do not go getting fussy with her. It annoys people, gets on their nerves, you know. Just go easy on the little things."

"I don't know what you mean, I'm sure!"

Lily smiled and continued her approach with a heavy tread to diffuse Hilda's indignation. She sat between them and thanked Hilda for the cup of tea she put in front of her.

"Milk, dear? It's not only us English, a lot of Canadians take it that way, too."

Magaly snorted and Lily said she loved tea with milk. She had never had it that way—even though her parents had been English, they drank only instant coffee on those rare occasions they drank anything nonalcoholic—but decided it tasted good, especially with the strong brew Hilda had made.

"Well, Lily, what will you do with yourself in the big city?" Hilda asked.

"I want to see as much as I can of the city, first of all. And I'm trying to write a romance novel. I don't suppose I'm very good at it, but I do enjoy my scribbling. Maybe I'll take a writing class later on. I might even look for a part-time job in a few months. Doing what, I don't know, but I'll see how things go."

"Well, just you be careful after dark. There's a killer loose, you know," Hilda whispered with some melodrama.

"Oh, do not be so silly, Hilda. He goes after little girls, not grown women, the filthy swine. I would give him something to think about if I got my hands on him, I can tell you!" Magaly said, her voice rising in volume and pitch and her clenched fist slamming on the table, making them jump.

"Why Magaly, I've never heard you talk like that before. Whatever's the matter?"

Hilda clearly disapproved of unseemly displays of passion. She seemed to have compressed herself into a smaller space; even her face had pinched tight. Lily sensed she was probably uncomfortable with any strong feelings, even her own.

"I think Magaly feels strongly about men who prey on children, and quite right, too. Perhaps she has known someone who has suffered, as I have." It came out stronger than Lily had intended. "They cause pain and suffering to the living as well as the dead. They should be shown no mercy."

The two old women looked at her, Magaly with appreciation and Hilda with uneasiness.

"Well, perhaps we should talk about something more cheerful," Lily said brightly. She hadn't meant to give so much of herself away so soon. And a fine one she was to talk about retribution, although she'd never gone after children.

Except the first kill, and that was for a special reason. An act of mercy.

"I tell you what, I noticed a nice little Italian restaurant just at the end of the road. Why don't you let me invite you both to dinner?"

"Oh, we couldn't possibly…" Hilda started to protest, only to be interrupted by Magaly who said, "You are very kind, that would be most wonderful."

"Is six-thirty convenient for you both? I'd like to lie down with a book for a couple of hours first, if that's all right," Lily said.

She smiled at them, pleased to see their excitement. She supposed they didn't get out much.

Their slow procession wended its way down the avenue that evening. The table was one of those with padded booth seats, and Lily suggested that she sit on the inside, and they could take the two outside seats. She knew it would take a Herculean effort to get them installed if they had to scoot all the way along the bench. It was hard enough for them to negotiate the inevitable meeting of table edges and hips and canes and other diners.

The menu produced dilemmas galore for Hilda—expense, foreign words, and whether they could eat as much as three courses. The waiter assured them that they could take any leftovers home. Hilda confided in a whisper that she didn't know if foreign food was good for her delicate digestion. Lily pointed out dishes that were not too rich and solved her embarrassment over expense by ordering the most costly veal entrée on the menu. Magaly didn't seem concerned about anything except enjoying the moment.

"I'm celebrating finding a new home," Lily said. "So I'm splurging tonight and I want you to order whatever you fancy. Shall we have some wine?"

An hour-and-a-half later, Hilda and Magaly were pink-cheeked and merry. At the end of the meal, they had to visit the ladies' room, of course, and Lily helped them navigate the obstacles on their way. She wondered if they could manage the walk home, but it was too short a distance for a taxi. She waited outside their stalls, smiling as she registered the contrast of Magaly's strong flowing stream, and Hilda's more refined tinkle on the edge of the bowl. When she got them outside with minor difficulties—only one waiter's shin bone assaulted by Hilda's cane, and only one wine glass swept to the floor because Magaly was roughly the same width as the aisle—they seemed easier in their gait and moved at a reasonable speed. They chatted and giggled about the people who lived on their street and, Lily felt, they made most of it up as they went along.

Magaly went straight over to her house and they waited to make sure she got inside safely with the doggie bag she clutched as if afraid she'd be mugged for it. When Hilda and Lily got home, Hilda said, "I'm going straight to bed, dear. I had such a lovely evening. Thanks ever so much, I can't think when I've had a nicer time."

"Goodnight, Hilda, so glad you enjoyed it, I did too. I'll just put your doggie bag in the fridge and then I'll come up. Would you like me to lock up?"

"Oh, would you? The key goes back on the table, and do top and bottom bolts, mind."

"Don't worry, I'll see to it. Goodnight."

Lily got into bed and picked up her Toronto guidebook. Where would she start? Maybe visit the CN Tower tomorrow, have lunch there, and then take the boat ride around the harbor. Then she'd spend the evening working on her book. She turned out the light and thought over the day. How comfortable she had been with those old ladies. She'd acted lighthearted in the restaurant and was surprised to be so moved by their excitement and pleasure. She felt better than she had in a long time, less burdened by the past. Perhaps she could shake it all off. Eventually.

She hoped her children were all right. Lucy and Justin would get over the thunderbolt that had struck their family, but she wasn't sure about Andrew. She must learn how to use the internet properly. Maybe she could find out about them that way. She'd heard you could find anything out about anyone on the internet.

She drifted off to sleep and dreamed of the children in their younger, happier days, laughing and playing on the beach. *All of a sudden she realized they were walking into the ocean and not even trying to swim, just striding deeper and deeper. She chased after them, trying to call out, but unable to utter a sound. They never turned back, just kept on going until the water closed over their heads. Someone held her arms and pulled her back. She couldn't see his face, but knew it was their dead father, Victor. "Let them go," he said, gently.*

Lily seemed tired and quiet at breakfast. Hilda tried to draw her out, but she answered with an icy politeness.

"Lily, I'd like to cook for you and Magaly one day next week. I had such a lovely time last night, I won't forget it for a long time. What day would be best for you, dear?"

"That's very kind. You pick the day. I'm free anytime."

Hilda carried on with a few remarks about the weather before giving up. *Lily got up on the wrong side of her bed this morning,* she huffed to herself. *Headache from the wine, perhaps.* She looked at Lily over her teacup. Her face looked, well, closed. It had been so open and friendly yesterday. This was a woman with problems.

Magaly hadn't visited the day after their dinner outing as she had spent the day at her daughter's house. Hilda decided to go over there for a change, although Magaly walked more easily than she did. They sat with their coffee in a breakfast nook in the kitchen that overlooked the garden. Magaly paid a gardener to come in once a week, but the flower display wasn't what it used to be. But then nothing was. The man just mowed the lawn and did a bit of weeding. He didn't have time to plant the annuals that used to be Magaly's pride and joy, and she could no longer stoop or kneel. There was a bird feeder that Magaly was still able to keep stocked, and Hilda loved watching the birds come and go. She had asked her son to get her one several times, but he always forgot. He had a lot on his mind, of course.

"Well, Hilda, how does it go with Lily?"

"Fine. She was very standoffish yesterday morning, looked tired and upset. She was all right this morning, though."

"Maybe she had a bad night, bad dreams perhaps."

"I didn't think of that. Why on earth should she have nightmares?"

"You never know, Hilda, you never know. She has got a past, that one."

"Oh, do you think so? I hope she'll work out."

"I think she will. I think she needs a place to call home. What did she do yesterday?"

"She told me about it this morning. She didn't come in until about seven, then went straight up to her room. She said she went to the CN Tower and had lunch in the cafeteria. She said she got a window table and liked looking down on planes taking off and landing from that little airport on the island down there. She said you can see the roofs of the other high-rises around. And there's a glass floor that you can stand on and look all the way down. Fancy that!" Hilda shuddered and took another sip. "I'd find it quite frightening being up that high. She said that after that she went on a boat tour around the harbor, and then took a long walk. She had dinner at an Italian restaurant and she said it was nothing special, not like the one we had together. She felt it was really a place for tourists, and didn't I think the neighborhood places were often better?"

"Well, she has not wasted no time, has she? I suppose she spent the evening reading."

"She said she would write a little bit of her book before going to sleep."

"I wonder what it is about? Did she say?"

"No, of course I asked, but she said it was too early to discuss it."

"And what will she do today?"

"She said she thought the Royal Ontario Museum and the Art Gallery of Ontario. From what I've heard, you can spend all week in just one of those. Did you see the news this morning? A second one. Shocking business."

Magaly puffed out her lips. "Well, when they find him, I hope he will spend a long, miserable life in his prison cell and suffer a long, painful death at the end. Men who interfere with little girls are bad enough, but to kill them, too? Poor, poor, parents." Her fists clenched again, like the other day.

Magaly's tone, so angry and full of sorrow, silenced Hilda. Could there be something in her past that wasn't quite right? Someone in the family, perhaps? Hilda shook off the distasteful thought and went back to watching the birds. She didn't like to talk about unpleasantness.

The autumn colors looked better than ever this year, although that splendid blurring of every possible shade of red and orange would soon turn to drab brown, and sunny blue skies to gray. Like their lives, which had melted from daylight to dusk in what seemed like an instant. It was hard, growing old. Hilda tried not to think too often of lost time, lost opportunities. Loss.

2

It was early November now and Hilda watched the most stubborn of the oak leaves drift and dance to earth. Such a shocking change in Lily's manner. How different from how she'd acted at their lovely Thanksgiving celebration only a few weeks ago. Their children had other plans, so Magaly and Hilda cooked a traditional dinner at Magaly's house for Lily. Lily had brought a bottle of wine and they got quite silly—well, she and Magaly had, as Lily was far too reserved to get silly. Hilda usually acted much more dignified, but in front of Magaly she could let her hair down, couldn't she? And in front of Lily, too.

When their children came, there was always some kind of tension—the dinner wasn't quite right, Hilda should sell the house and move, Magaly should invest in a burglar alarm company her son wanted to start—always something. This year, they'd just had a nice time together. Strange that

Lily had been surprised by the date. She'd seemed to think that Thanksgiving was in November, like in America. Maybe they hadn't ever celebrated up there in Manitoba. And Lily had been in a really good mood, not like last night.

Magaly knocked and came through the back door into the kitchen.

"Good morning, Hilda. How are you this morning?"

"Oh, well enough, well enough."

"I just saw Lily leave. Where's she going today?"

"I don't know, didn't ask. I think I'd better watch my step with that one."

"What is the matter? What has happened?"

"Well, you know how she said she preferred to clean her own room and make her own bed? When she was out yesterday, I left her clean sheets on her bed as usual. But she didn't come back for hours, so at seven o'clock I decided to make up her bed, do her a favor so she'd be able to just go to bed if she came in late. I didn't hear her come in, and she gave me quite a start when she slammed the bedroom door like that." Hilda's voice almost sobbed, so she took a deep breath to steady herself. "Her face got all twisted and white. She looked like a madwoman! And her eyes! I was scared, I can tell you. She said, 'I thought I told you I would see to my own room! I don't like people in my things!' I was so shocked, I just said, 'I was only trying to help.' I left the room and came downstairs to make a cup of tea. Gave me quite a turn. What a betrayal after I've been so nice and when I was only trying to do her a kindness."

"Oh, Hilda, what a strange thing for that nice woman to do! I wonder if there is something in her room that should not be. Have you seen her since?"

"Yes, half an hour or so later, she came down to the kitchen and apologized. She said she understood completely how

I'd only wanted to do something nice for her and admitted she had behaved very badly." Hilda frowned and looked at Magaly, still bewildered. "She told me some story about a landlady she used to have who always went through her things and read a murder mystery she was trying to write. She said her landlady thought the story was a journal that she'd written about herself and threatened to call the police. She said she threw the story away and moved to another apartment. But she just didn't want any more misunderstandings. I told her I wouldn't dream of snooping about in her things. Then she said she was sorry again for her outburst. It all sounds very farfetched to me, I must say."

"I do think that is a little strange," said Magaly. "I wonder what is in her room that she does not want you to see."

"Well, nothing I could find, uh…" Hilda broke off, blushing.

"Hilda, you are the sly one! When did you have a look? And what did you find?"

"Last week. I knew she was going to a matinee at the harbor front and wouldn't be back for hours. I didn't find anything much. Part of her story, but nothing very spicy. No letters, no nothing. A small locked briefcase in the armoire. That must be where she keeps her passport, because it wasn't in the chest of drawers, you see, and I'm sure she must have one if she's an American."

"Interesting!"

"Well, anyway, I have a right to know who I've got living in my house, don't I?" Hilda averred with self-righteous indignation. "You can't be too careful these days!"

"No, Hilda, you are quite right, I am sure. But I would not do any more spying if I were you."

"It wasn't spying, it was just being cautious! Why do you always have to put things in such a bad light?"

"It is as you say, Hilda, just being cautious," Magaly said with an irritating smirk. "What I find interesting is what she does not have. She is like a woman with no past, and that means she has quite a past, one she would sooner forget about."

"Perhaps her husband's family was nasty, and she doesn't want them to find her. Perhaps her husband isn't dead at all!"

"More likely, I think, something before that. No family, no friends before Manitoba? Well, whoever she is, I think she is all right now. Just let her alone. She likes being in your home, that is for sure." Magaly stopped and peered at her. "You are not worried are you, Hilda?"

Hilda breathed deeply, hesitating a little. Her hands clutched her cup like little bird claws. "Well, not really. But you should have seen her face. I felt she was out of control. I thought she hated me enough to hurt me at that moment! She certainly wasn't very ladylike."

Magaly patted her arm. "She calmed down and apologized though, did she not?" Her voice was softer, gentle. "I think she is fond of you in her own way. She will not hurt you, Hilda. Do not worry yourself."

"It's a funny life, isn't it? Running around the city all day and scribbling in her notebook all evening."

"It is more than we do, Hilda, much more than we do."

"Yes. But when we were her age, we were busy with our families," Hilda said.

"She does not have a family, though, does she? How old do you think she is?"

"I don't know, fifty, do you think?"

"Something like that, although she looks very good for her age."

"Well, she doesn't have children, does she? That's what puts the age on you," Hilda said with a sigh.

The two friends nodded at this last remark and looked into their coffee cups as if seeking to read their fortunes. For them, good fortune would be to spend their old age in comfort and dignity, and they knew that would not happen if they were left to the mercy of their children's efforts.

"Magaly, do you ever think what will happen when we can't manage a house anymore? What will you do?" Hilda asked.

"You know, I have been thinking. There is an apartment complex I read about where it is all for old people. They have staff if you need help, and they have a dining room where you can eat if you do not feel like cooking. And there is a grocery store right next door. How convenient is that? I thought a small two-bedroom apartment would be nice. I figured I could afford to move there if I sell the house. And you, Hilda, what about you?"

"I've just worried about it, but I haven't heard of that place." Hilda paused and looked puzzled. "What do you want with two bedrooms?"

"I could get that or a smaller one, but I would like to have my best friend share it. It might be lonely without her!"

"You mean me? You'd really want to live with me?" Hilda felt her face light up; she couldn't help it.

"Of course, do I have another best friend? We could go halves."

"Oh, Magaly!"

Hilda was overrun by confusion and emotion. Magaly thought enough of her that she wanted to spend her last years with Hilda. But they'd have to share the kitchen. They'd have to agree on a lot of things. Of course, they wouldn't have to cook much. Whose sofa would they take? They'd have privacy in their bedrooms. They'd have company, always.

It could work. She'd have to think it all through and know more about the money side of it.

"Let us go and look at the place next week," Magaly said.

"Yes, I'd have to know a lot more about it. Look before you leap, my father always used to say," Hilda said primly.

Hilda knew Magaly wasn't fooled by this cool response. She had sharp eyes that noticed everything and she'd have seen the sudden tears in her eyes and, try as she might, she couldn't keep the emotion off her face. She was counting on Hilda to go. And why not?

In early December, a thin frosting of snow crusted the ground. Hilda was afraid to go out as she was terrified of falling and breaking a hip, often the beginning of the end for old people. But Magaly wasn't afraid of anything, and Hilda watched her stomp across the road very carefully, her feet in their boat-like lace-ups placed carefully down flat at each step. Her face was blotchy red from the wind that seemed to blow straight down from Lake Ontario, and cold air swept around her as she shed her overcoat and scarf.

"Hah! So it starts, the weather," Magaly said as she collapsed onto her usual chair (which Hilda had had reinforced a few years before).

"Yes, I hate the winter. Well, I hope this is the last winter in our houses. An apartment will be much better, much easier." Hilda perched on the edge of her seat.

"Yes, that has taken a burden off both of our minds. We will have to decide what to give away, what to sell, what we will put in the living room. But think of all the stuff we will not be cleaning!"

"Yes, but I like my things. I've had them for a very long time. It's so hard to decide." Hilda was saddened by the inevitable shedding of a lifetime's careful acquisitions.

"You will manage. Anyhow, have you seen the news this morning? Another poor child!"

"Yes, the third. Just cast aside like rubbish. I can't understand how someone can get away with it without getting found out. I don't understand it. You'd think everyone could tell what he's like just by looking at him!"

"Oh, Hilda. He probably just looks regular and no one has any idea what he does."

"That's very frightening! Just think what that poor mite must have gone through before she died."

"Just think what the poor parents are going through now," said Magaly.

"They've rounded up all those people who do things to children, and apparently it's not any of them. You know, some of those sex offenders, as they call them these days, have been attacked. One was even stoned yesterday. He's still unconscious."

"Serves him right. I would hang the fellow on a lamppost by his balls and leave him there until he rots!" Magaly shouted.

"Shhh!" Hilda was scandalized. She'd never heard such words from her friend. Thank heavens the windows were closed. "Well, I never! What a thing to say!"

Then she noticed Magaly's closed eyes and high color, higher, for sure, than her own. Magaly clenched her fists and breathed heavily, her chest heaving.

"Are you all right, my dear?" she asked as she patted her friend's hand, wondering if Magaly was going to have a heart attack.

Magaly took a deep breath and opened her eyes. "Yes, Hilda, I am all right. I just hate people who do such wicked things. Hate them with all my heart."

"Let's change the subject," said Hilda. "This is causing you too much upset. It's not good for you."

"Yes, you are right. What is Lily up to these days?"

"You know that bookshop on St. Clair? I can never remember its name."

"I know it. In fact, I know the owner. She came into our restaurant all the time in the old days. It is called Wendy's Words."

"Yes, I knew it was something silly like that. Anyway, the shop has a part-time opening for an assistant, and Lily said she might apply. She said she's going to slow down on the sightseeing now. She can just see one or two things each week in her spare time. She said she finds the idea of being around all those books very attractive. And she could walk to work."

"Well, that is good. Have there been any repeats of her outburst since that time?"

"No, I'd almost forgotten it. No, everything has been going very well."

"Well, tell her I will call Wendy Plummer and put in a good word for her if she wants."

"I'm sure she'd be very grateful, Magaly. By the way, Lily has been asking about Christmas. Do you have any plans?"

"None yet. What is she thinking of?" Magaly asked.

"She said she would like to help me do the dinner for the three of us, that she would do the shopping, and that perhaps any of your or my children who are free could just come to my house to eat. What do you think?" asked Hilda.

"I think that would be very nice. None of us want to be alone. And if our children have other things to do, we can be very merry, the three of us," said Magaly with solemn emphasis. "These young ones do not want to cook the dinner, but I think some of them will come if they think they are getting a free dinner that they do not have to be responsible for. I will help you, too. And I will make a Hungarian chestnut pudding."

"Oh, thank you," Hilda said, relieved. She was not averse to solitude in general, but Christmastime was another thing altogether.

<h1 style="text-align:right">3</h1>

W endy Plumber fumbled for her keys in the black hole of her purse, tried to keep her long, gray hair from blowing into her eyes, and inevitably dropped the newspaper that had been clutched under her arm. The chill wind off the lake penetrated even down to this part of town today. She found the keys at last, opened the barred door, and entered her bookstore's familiar fuggy warmth. She hoped everyone would be on time, as she had several interviews scheduled for the open position she had advertised. It was one of those "and any duties that may be required" positions, as hers was a small bookstore and she needed everyone to be able to cover for each other—except Peter Bachman, the bookkeeper. She'd hired Steve in desperation a couple of weeks before, but he had no literary competence, and probably only read rock magazines—or whatever his generation called their music these days. She hoped to find someone who at least read bestsellers, if not the classics. Steve could barely do his own job, let alone take on extra tasks.

"Morning Peter," she called as she saw him shuffle to his desk. His musky cologne wafted after him.

"Morning."

Peter rarely looked anyone in the face, but he was competent, quite the best bookkeeper she'd had in years, since her father died, in fact. When she'd opened the store twenty years before, her parents had been wonderful, her father dealing with the finances and her mother helping with everything else. It was largely thanks to them that the business had got its solid start. She'd had time for fun, then, but now taking care of her business and the large house she'd inherited consumed her. She didn't know how much longer she could go on. The big chains didn't even need to buy up the small businesses as their volume discounts simply crushed them into bankruptcy. However, there wasn't another bookstore within walking distance, or even an easy streetcar ride to Wendy's Words, so she still enjoyed a loyal local following.

Nancy came in next, stopping outside Wendy's office with her usual cheery greeting. Wendy, who was never perky in the mornings, had to make a conscious effort to respond in kind. Wendy shouldn't have minded this small concession to a good employee, but she did. She stared down into her coffee cup and willed her irritation to drain away. "Never start a day by sowing bad seeds, my dear," her mother used to say.

"Morning boss!" shouted Steve as he lurched by, a few minutes late as usual. He watched too many bad American movies and tried to emulate those street-smart punks to impress his friends. Her irritation rose again as she anticipated his baggy pants and slangy nonsense-talk. She closed her eyes, swiveled her chair so her back was to the door, and sipped her coffee, letting its fragrance permeate her mind and its caffeine her bloodstream.

Nancy appeared at her door again to announce the first applicant, a fragile-looking man, probably about forty, tall, thin, and stooped, and completely bald. His glasses roosted halfway down his nose and he peered over them with wide, frightened eyes.

"Good morning. Mr. Edgington, isn't it?"

He started as if poked with a cattle prod. "Er, yes. Robert Edgington," he said as he extended his hand. Wendy endured his clammy grasp, which he gave no sign of releasing until she could stand it no more and pulled her own hand back.

"Tell me about yourself, Mr. Edgington. Have you worked in a bookstore before?"

"Well, yes, in my last job."

"Why did you leave?"

"I had a spot of bad health, and they weren't very nice about it."

One of those. "What do you like about working in a bookstore?"

"I love books. I read all the time. My apartment is full of them, right up to the ceiling in some rooms. I can't bear to get rid of any of them. Of course, they get dreadfully dusty, but I'm not strong, you see, I can't lift and carry heavy weights."

"Well, Mr. Edgington, you would have to be able to lift boxes of books here, although no individual box is very heavy. And you'd have to help unpack, sort, and shelve them, too. In fact, everyone who works here has to be able to do whatever is needed, including me."

"Oh, I could help customers, and I can use the cash registers and the credit card machines, but I wouldn't want to lift things. My mother always discouraged me from straining myself, you know, and I think she was quite right. I have to be careful of my health. I have a weak chest, and I get back-aches a lot."

These last confidences were imparted in a breathy voice as he leaned farther and farther across Wendy's desk, wafting bad breath and earnestness into her face as she leaned back in a matching arc.

"Mr. Edgington," Wendy said in her take-charge voice, her chair precarious on its two back legs, "I don't think this is the right place for you. My store is a small business and, except for the bookkeeper, we can't afford to have employees who can't do some of the heavier work."

"Well, I can do bookkeeping. Why don't you let me do that and let the other person work on the harder things?"

"Oh, I couldn't possibly do that. Peter has been doing a wonderful job, and that's what he was hired for, after all."

"Well," said Robert Edgington as he unfurled himself from the chair, "I don't think I'd want to work in a place where people aren't flexible." His voice had become high and peevish. "I need to work in a place where there's some consideration for my health."

"Mr. Edgington, we all need to be flexible here, and I cannot make exceptions."

The man turned abruptly and left, his indignant chin held so high he sailed along, quite oblivious to his surroundings, until he tripped on the store threshold. Wendy watched through the window as he scurried down the street; even the sight of his retreating back riled her beyond reason. After she'd washed his slimy touch off her hands and splashed cool water over her face, she went to the back room where Nancy and Steve were unpacking some new arrivals.

"I gather he didn't suit," Nancy said with a giggle.

"Dreadful man. Said he was too fragile to lift anything. Even suggested I let him do bookkeeping and make Peter do the other work." She was startled to see Peter's usually deadpan face shoot up with a look of palpable anger. "I told him that was out of the question, that Peter does a wonderful job and that was what he had been hired to do." Peter's face relaxed back down into surliness and paperwork. "And he had the nerve to accuse *me* of being inflexible!"

Nancy and Steve laughed, and she, finally seeing the funny side of it, laughed too, laughing harder as she had a sudden mental image of Robert Edgington trapped on the floor of his apartment under an avalanche of books. Her good mood subsided when the next interview called to cancel. She'd accepted a job at the huge bookstore downtown. Hell and damnation! The last person wasn't due until eleven, so she made a new pot of coffee. Steve and Nancy were talking about the killer who had been preying on little girls. Two had been found raped and strangled, only nine and ten years old.

"I'm so worried about my two," said Nancy. "Cindy gets so mad at me when I won't let her out alone at night, but it's really scary, and she should be scared if she had any sense, which she doesn't, of course. Kids seem to think bad things only happen to other people."

"How old is she?" asked Steve.

"Sixteen."

"Well, he seems to like them younger. He's a real pervert," said Steve. "It's the little one you want to worry about."

Peter cursed under his breath as he spilled some of the coffee he was pouring for himself. Wendy waited while he wiped off the counter before pouring her own—she knew better than to offer to help him.

"I think we all need to be careful. What do you think, Peter?" she asked in an attempt to bring him into the circle. He just looked at her and shrugged and went back to his desk. Steve rolled his eyes, and Nancy frowned. Wendy ran her fingers through her hair.

The doorbell alerted them to the arrival of a customer and Wendy went to the front of the shop. "Can I help you?" she asked.

"I stopped in to introduce myself." Nice voice, educated, firm handshake. "Name's Cecil Blount, and I just moved to Toronto from Kitchener. I was teaching writing at Lambert College until they downsized the English department. I've set up quite a business tutoring and teaching online, and I wanted to see if any of the bookstores would like to let me use their space to give evening workshops. It would help me and maybe bring new customers into the store, too."

"Let's talk," Wendy replied, intrigued. "Why don't we go back to my office?"

Cecil was about forty-five, she reckoned, and attractive in a quiet, bookish sort of way. They talked for over an hour, and Wendy agreed to host a writing workshop on Tuesday evenings. Well-spoken and gentle in manner, personable— she would go so far as to say charming—he should get along well with the students. Wendy went to tell Peter.

"Peter, I've agreed to let that man who was just in give a writing workshop once a week for ten weeks, starting in mid-January. We agreed on a $150 fee per student, $75 each for the store and him. We're hoping for at least eight participants. I reckon it'll bring extra customers into the store. The thing is, we'll have to advertise. Can you figure out some costs for me?"

Peter fixed her with his gray pebble eyes while she spoke, and now abruptly dropped them as he said, "Sure."

Wendy, irritated by his surliness, went back to her office and worked on next month's orders. Maybe she'd sit in on the writing class, even participate. Why not?

Nancy called out, "There's someone to see you, Wendy."

"Oh, goodness, is it eleven o'clock already? Could you show her to my office, please? I just want to wash my hands."

Wendy looked in the mirror, something she rarely did. She'd get a haircut soon, a good one. She hadn't paid any attention to her appearance for years and realized she looked downright dowdy.

The woman regarded a spot just over Wendy's right shoulder. She had greeted Wendy cordially enough in a well-modulated voice and sat with her knees together, ankles crossed and hands resting on her purse. She seemed preternaturally still.

"Well, Mrs. Porter, why have you applied for a position here?"

"I would like a part-time job and the ad mentioned half days. I love to read, and I think I would enjoy this environment. I may as well tell you at once that I have no references. I was married and lived on a farm in Manitoba for many years and didn't work. I was very lonely there, so after my husband died I came to Toronto to find a new life."

"I see. I must tell you that all the employees have to be willing to perform any of the tasks that need doing, whether it be unpacking books and shelving them or assisting customers. Does that bother you?"

"Not at all," Lily replied, finally looking Wendy in the face with an intense gaze she found disconcerting.

Wendy went on to talk about the job, hours, and pay while Lily moved back to gazing over her shoulder. Then she went on to tell her about Cecil and the writing workshop.

"That's excellent. I'm trying to write a romance novel and I've been thinking about taking a class. I could do it right here," Lily said.

"I think I must advertise to get enough students. Advertising is so expensive these days."

"Why not put posters in the windows and fliers at the cash register? You might get most of the students that way," suggested Lily. "And I'm sure some of the other local businesses wouldn't mind displaying your materials."

"You know, that's a great idea. I'll start work on it tomorrow. Let me introduce you to the rest of the staff," Wendy said, rising.

Wendy watched Lily as she made the rounds of the back room, noting her pleasant manner and the positive reactions of Steve and Nancy. Peter looked up, nodded, and looked down again without a word. The phone rang in her office, and she beckoned Lily to follow her.

"Oh, Magaly, how nice to hear from you. No, she's still here."

The call, one-sided for the most part, went on for five minutes, and Wendy was sure Lily could hear Magaly's voice from where she was sitting, judging by the small smile playing around the corners of her mouth. She finally ended the call and looked at Lily.

"Well, Magaly gave you a glowing reference! In fact, she was, how shall I put it..."

"Impassioned?" Lily finished with a husky laugh, which sounded incongruous.

"Yes, I think that's a good way of putting it." Wendy laughed, too, a little too loudly. The woman had her off-key, veering from sharp to flat.

"I expect she told you that I rent a room from her best friend, Hilda, who lives across the street from her. We've become quite a little family, and I'm very fond of them both."

"It seems the feeling is reciprocated. I would like to offer you the position—if you're interested, that is."

"Yes, I think I could be very content here. When would you like me to start?"

"We're closed on Sunday and Monday, so how about Tuesday?"

"Fine, and please call me Lily."

Wendy chewed on her pencil as she mulled over the interview. Catching sight of her ragged nails, she decided she'd take an afternoon off to go to the hairdressers next week, since she'd have some extra help. She must get a good haircut and a manicure. It was high time she had some new clothes, too. The blue stocking look had gone out years back, and was even less flattering at forty-two than it had been at twenty.

Lily was a strange one, for sure, somewhat reserved, although she had spoken pleasantly enough to the others. She had a professional demeanor and would probably do well with the customers. She seemed intelligent, so should pick up the cash register and credit card paraphernalia without difficulty. *All in all, a good choice*, Wendy decided. Not that there was much choice. It was just that stillness, the unwillingness to meet her eye one minute, and then the strange stare that seemed to go right through you the next. Well, time would tell. Maybe she'd go to the Eaton Centre after the shop closed and look at clothes. Wendy felt almost cheerful. People might laugh at her behind her back—mutton dressed as lamb, they'd say. *Too bad!*

Wendy had told Lily that Cecil wanted the students to have made a good start on their stories, at least ten pages or so, so that the class would have something to work on from day one. They were to leave a copy of their work in the shop two weeks before the first class—a month away to be sure, but she didn't have the self-confidence to dash something off— and Lily was glad to have a deadline to make her get started in earnest. She had lain in bed at night with the lights out for a week as she worked out what she wanted to write about in her romance novel. She'd decided on a private school, based on her knowledge of the Salton Academy where her daughter Lucy had gone from kindergarten through twelfth grade. Victor had decided that the boys would be fine in the public school system, but that his little girl should stay in a more protected environment. He never saw that his daughter was a little tiger who could take care of herself under almost any circumstances. Much more competent than her brother Julian, for example, a gentle, idealistic, and artistic boy; he'd become a musician. She supposed he still was, hoped so. And poor Andrew, sensitive to a fault. Well, it did no good to think about the children now. That part of her life was closed off. Completely.

Lily chewed her pencil and read what she'd written so far.

> Laura and her fellow teachers sat in the school auditorium waiting for the staff meeting to begin. It had been announced only yesterday, and attendance was mandatory. They'd all been complaining, some because sports practices

had been canceled, and those teachers not involved with sports because they had to stay late. Lazy bunch, Laura thought, as she watched them grousing. The buzz got louder as everyone's speculations got wilder by the minute. Finally, the Chairman of the Board, Emanuel Davies, strode onto the stage, took possession of the podium, and looked around at the sea of expectant faces in front of him, much as a shark might survey his luncheon menu.

"Good afternoon, ladies and gentlemen. I expect you're wondering what this is all about, so I'll get right to it. Our headmaster, Miles Upton, has resigned his post as Headmaster of the Mackie Academy, effective immediately. I am not at liberty to divulge the circumstances surrounding his decision, but he would wish you to know that it was not a course of action he chose lightly. He has already moved from the campus house. In fact, has moved out of state. He did not wish to go through any painful goodbyes, but sends you all his very best wishes." He paused to give the buzz a chance to die down. Laura saw that people were excited rather than dismayed— Miles Upton had not been popular with the faculty or, lately, with the parents.

"You will be surprised to know that we have been fortunate enough to appoint a new headmaster already, and I would like to introduce him to you now. Dr. Gary

Woodbury was most recently headmaster at the Leston School in Pennsylvania—a fine school as I'm sure you all know. He resigned his post there about eighteen months ago, as his wife was very ill and needed constant care. Tragically, she passed away last year. Dr. Woodbury now feels ready to reenter his chosen profession, and we feel very lucky to have him at this difficult time. Dr. Woodbury, please come to the podium."

Laura's head was reeling. It was unheard of to appoint a school head without a lengthy search by a committee of faculty, parents, administration members, and board members.

Lucy's school board fired the headmaster once—or, rather, chose not to renew his contract. Victor got himself in the middle of it, defending the man and protesting this ungrateful treatment after so many years of faithful service, and so on. He'd come home after meetings fired up, practically foaming, relating who said what, some parents screaming for blood on one side, others infuriated by the removal of the glad-handing confrontation-averse malleable teddy bear they'd come to rely on. The guy was an idiot, good at schmoozing donors, good at soothing ruffled parents, not so good when it came to finance and other knotty problems. Lily couldn't be bothered with all the hoopla. The deputy turned out to be the better bet and was soon confirmed. Handsome, too.

The Deputy Head, Tina Golan, was perfectly capable of filling in and, in Laura's opinion, would have made a very good Head. Laura had not liked Miles Upton. Too fond of leering at the female staff, he was rather an oily character. His interest in academia was shallow at best, but she supposed that the headmaster of private schools these days had to be able to administer large budgets and facilities and be good at fundraisers. Almost impossible to find someone good at it all.

A man walked onto the stage and shook hands with his new boss before taking his place behind the podium. Another shock. This man was drop-dead gorgeous. He stood well over six feet and had thick, dark hair swept back from a face that had a rugged, outdoorsy look. She couldn't see the color of his eyes, but supposed they must be brown. She felt her breath catch and heard little murmurs from the other females in the room. Looking around, she saw the men applauded politely, but not as enthusiastically as the women, and most wore slight frowns.

Did women really react like that when faced with a handsome man? Lily hadn't met many very handsome men, but on those rare occasions, had tended to distrust them. People—both men and women—who were very good-looking tended to rely on those looks to get them through life and never developed much depth of character. But she did remember some friends at a coffee morning gushing over a handsome guest artist who had performed operatic arias with the Salton Symphony the evening before. She had not thought him that talented, but these other women, who had obviously been fantasizing about him, dubbed him brilliant.

Lily had no idea what that felt like—she'd never been bowled over by anyone in her life. She knew girls in school had sometimes giggled about rock stars and movie actors in their little cliques, but she had never been part of those groups because nearly every time she moved to another foster home, she had to move to another school. And her lack of family and threadbare clothing had set her apart, although, thank God, the story of her family troubles never got out. Yes, these women were a sheltered lot and would probably melt at the prospect of having a rugged academic in their midst.

She'd have to give the man his nice little speech at this point, but she'd write that later. First, she'd write about their first meeting, and she'd follow the rules of the genre. Lily stopped chewing her pencil and began writing again.

It was mid-November, so the days were getting short. Although only five o'clock, it was already dusk. Laura had brought her book bag with her to the meeting, so went straight to her car. She was lost in thought as she considered the upheaval they would all have to go through, and she didn't see the figure coming out of the side door of the arts center until she collided with him. Her bag emptied all over the sidewalk, and, apparently, his coffee emptied all over him.

In spite of the angry curse, she recognized the voice.

"I am so sorry," she cried. "Oh, I've ruined your coat."

"Don't worry," he said. "It will come out with dry cleaning. Do you usually walk around in a fog?"

"I'm sorry," she said, cramming her books back into her bag. "I was just thinking about tomorrow's classes, and, to be honest, the changes to come at school."

"Don't worry too much about changes," he said, still mopping himself off with a handkerchief. "It's very possible that nothing much needs changing. Or would you disagree?"

"Well, there's always room for improvement, isn't there?"

"When we have our meeting, I'll expect you to be able to offer something a little more profound than a platitude," he replied.

Lily used to make tart comments all the time at home, or rather Rose, as she was known then, did. She'd taken care to be charming socially, leaving the tongue-lashings to Susan, one of her Salton Symphony friends. Former friends. That sharpness came out of her more and more over the years, but usually at home. It started with Lucy when she became a teen and went through the inevitable angst and defiance. Victor always defended her, so came in for his share. Lucy buttressed herself with so much anger it rubbed off on anyone within reach. She never quite overcame that. Never said sorry. Neither did Rose.

> Laura stammered, "Well, sorry again, I'll look where I'm going in the future."
> "Excellent. And what do you teach?"
> "Upper School English."
> "Well, goodnight, then."
> "Goodnight, Dr. Woodbury."
> "Oh, and you are?"
> "Laura Jones."
> "Ah!"
> What did he mean, "Ah?" Did he mean he'd heard about her? Maybe Tina had given him a rundown of the entire faculty, but that would be unlikely in a school of this size. Anyway, she'd never done anything to get herself talked about. Or maybe he meant he'd be sure to remember the name of the stupid teacher who'd knocked coffee all over him. Laura was mortified. What a way to start off with the new headmaster. She could feel she was still flushed and would probably get red-faced again the next time she met him. She hoped she could avoid making a fool of herself next time.

Well, that was the first meeting of the hero and heroine over and done with. There had to be awkwardness at the first meeting and further misunderstandings between them, even as they fell in love. All kinds of obstacles had to be placed in their way. That was the formula. This Lily knew because she'd read at least twenty romance novels in Syracuse while she lay low until she could safely cross the border. She'd found them tedious after the first few, but was having fun thinking through one of her own. She'd done a bit of scribbling in Syracuse, but couldn't settle on a theme. She felt too edgy in those days for writing, but she was quite settled in with Hilda now and wanted to get on with it.

She wasn't good enough yet to write a literary novel, and thrillers and mysteries were too close to the bone. It would have made a much more exciting story if she could kill off the handsome young man, but such gritty goings-on didn't belong in a romance novel—only in real life. Anyway, having experienced the thrill of killing firsthand, writing about it would be no fun at all—and dangerous, perhaps, as most people wouldn't know how good it could feel, and didn't want to. They might wonder how she knew. Although not necessarily. People imagined feelings for their books all the time. Look at the romance aspects of her novel, all gleaned from books she'd read about what other people claimed other people felt and did. Science fiction didn't interest her, and she didn't feel like doing the research to write a historical novel. That left romance. She knew there was a good market for romance paperbacks, and maybe she'd be successful, although she'd have to avoid having her picture taken. Writing was solitary work, just the thing for Lily.

There'd have to be a love scene or two. Heaven knows she'd read enough about it to get it right. She'd had her moments, although not too many. Maybe she could fantasize her way through a scene. It might be rather fun. A glass of wine or two should help loosen up her imagination. Muscles must ripple and warmth would flow through bloodstreams. She didn't have to be original, just catch the edges of her readers' fantasies. Some of the novels she'd read could have pulled her into a dreamland she wasn't keen on visiting, so she hadn't let it happen. Her ambitions would center around the structure of her writing. She didn't have to get hooked on her imagination, just find a way to make others get caught up in it.

She'd done enough writing for one night. She'd seen an ad where you could buy a computer and have a lesson on the spot and made up her mind to get one next weekend. Between that and the user manual, she should be able to manage. She wasn't a bad typist. Of course, getting on the internet would take more instruction, and there was the complication of a phone line. The important thing now was word processing so she could type, edit, and print her stories. Later, she'd figure out how to find her way around the internet so she could keep track of Salton and her children.

As Lily was undressing, she caught sight of herself in the mirror. She'd kept her figure even though she never exercised now, but she didn't eat much and walked a lot. As she turned this way and that, she decided she was still attractive, and she'd always had good posture. Not that it mattered. She liked to look nice, but wasn't interested in luring a man. She'd finished with all that. She had to be alone and keep her own counsel. She would never want to answer to anyone again. Lily pulled her nightdress over her head and climbed into bed. It was cold tonight, and she wished her bed was next to the radiator. Hilda had shown her a hot water bottle and told her she could get one like it in the drugstore. She wished she had done that. Tea with milk and a hot water bottle! She'd be eating crumpets at teatime next.

She turned off the lamp, snuggled under the duvet, and closed her eyes. She ought to think through some love scenes. She didn't feel she could submit love scenes for class, but the memories from all those paperbacks should set her on the right path.

Laura rested her head on his chest, the taut muscles surprisingly soft under her cheek. She felt his cheek brushing the top of her head, his lips grazing her forehead, and gasped as warmth flooded through her. He raised her chin and brought his lips down on hers, crushing them in his passion. She could feel...

Lily's eyes snapped open. How much was too much? She'd have to remember how other romance authors dealt with sex. A lot more bluntly than they had twenty years ago. She should go to sleep now. She wasn't in the mood for this stuff. She closed her eyes and set her mind on the speech Dr. Woodbury should give to the faculty, but her mind wouldn't cooperate.

...with a passion she'd never known possible, and rose to a dizzying crescendo together. They stayed in each other's arms, sated, as their pulses calmed. He kissed her again, gently, this time. "I love you, Gary," she murmured.
"I love you, too, Lily," she heard as she drifted into sleep.

4

Lily turned over the closed sign and waited for the other four class members to arrive. She felt jittery, but face it, a rank amateur had to expect her work to be torn apart. She looked over at Cecil, sitting at the end of the table they'd cleared, Wendy sitting on his right. She looked flushed and … what? Agitated? She'd had her hair cut and tinted, and wore a new outfit Lily had never seen before—tweed skirt, soft green wool sweater, and, ye gods, a manicure! Lipstick, too, discrete, but how the color lit up her face. Wendy liked Cecil. Did he realize? Cecil read some papers, and made notes, taking no notice whatever of the fluttering heart next to him. She was in for a letdown.

A couple of young women hesitated outside the door. Lily opened it and said, "Are you here for the writing class?"

"Yes, is that him?" asked one of them, peering inside, pointing. Her companion giggled suddenly, then suppressed it with a cough.

"Yes." These two would be tiresome. "Names?"

"I'm Maureen, she's Angela." Lily checked them off her list.

"Well, come in and sit down. We've got two more coming."

Soon Ruby and Carol arrived, middle-aged and tense. Cecil didn't bother to look up until everyone was seated. Wendy introduced him and asked everyone to introduce themselves and say why they came to the class and what kind of things they were writing, or would like to write.

"I'll start with myself. My name is Wendy and I own this store. I am writing a murder mystery set in a bookstore." She nodded at the woman next to her.

"Maureen. I'm writing a science fiction novel and I want to get it published." Lily, seated on the other side of Cecil, though she heard a faint harrumph.

"I'm Angela. I haven't started anything. I want to write a romance novel about a handsome doctor and this nurse and, you know, they fall in love and all. Only I don't know where to start. I dropped off a few paragraphs, a love scene, but I just wrote whatever came into my head after a date with my boyfriend." She giggled and Cecil sighed. Everyone smiled politely.

"My name is Ruby. My grandfather emigrated from Scotland and founded a shoe factory. I want to write his story."

"I'm Carol. I'm writing a historical mystery set in Toronto in 1900."

"I'm Lily. I am writing a romance novel set in a private school in the US"

"Well, well." Cecil looked around the table, smirking. "What a diverse and ambitious little group we have here. I have marked up your submissions and will pass them out at the end of next week's class. Wendy made enough copies for everyone. You will receive a copy of everyone's work—Wendy, please pass them out. You are to read them all and mark them up and be ready to discuss them next week."

They did a few exercises to streamline prose that was clumsy and hard to understand. Cecil went on to talk about free writing, and made them all write without stopping for fifteen minutes. It could be something true or made up. He gave them a prompt, "I've never been so scared…" He told them to close their eyes for a couple of minutes and think about it. He watched them like a hawk, rapping out a reprimand if he saw someone take her pen off the paper or, God forbid, scratch something out.

"I'm going to ask you to read your work now. And you will be quite surprised that it is not as incoherent as you might expect."

Some of the older women flexed their fingers and massaged their wrists. Lily hoped he wouldn't call on her. He turned to her.

"Let's hear from you, Lily."

"Er, okay. This is fiction and I got the idea from a TV program I saw a couple of months ago."

The story was about two sisters, one sixteen and one fourteen, who came home one day to find that the landlord had locked them out of their apartment. The rent had not been paid, and he'd seen their mother leaving with a suitcase earlier in the day. The teenagers hit the streets and the younger sister (the narrator) was taken away by a man from child services. No one could know this was her own story, but it reopened a wound she'd thought healed.

"You seem uncomfortable, Lily," said Cecil, looking at her closely. "It was very good, by the way, and shows how strong emotion lends itself to good storytelling. As long as you don't get carried away, of course, and become melodramatic." He looked at her even more closely. He'd caught it. *Control your face, compose yourself.*

They went around the table, and the stories were pretty tame in comparison. Lily couldn't wait to get home. After everyone had left, Lily helped Wendy tidy up, ready for the morning.

"You write very well, Lily," said Wendy. "I can't wait to read your story."

"Oh, it's just a romance, nothing earthshaking," Lily replied. "Nothing particularly dramatic."

She refused Wendy's offer of a ride home. She needed to walk off her agitation. Where was that woman, the slut who left two girls to sink or swim in a swamp like Hell's Kitchen? Maybe she should look for her. But then what? With any luck, she was dead already.

A week later, after the second class, Lily fell into bed exhausted after suffering through two hours of exercises and critiques. Cecil had a way of making even a compliment sound like a sneer. He'd pretty much torn everyone's work apart—for good reason, she had to admit—although Lily had come off comparatively lightly. She wondered how many students would return next week, as a couple definitely left with tears in their eyes. She'd turned in her next piece, although it would have helped to have her critique ahead of time. Oh well, she was a tough bird. How surprising that she should feel so nervous waiting for her turn and how important to her it was to have her writing appreciated. All the students had been very kind (and they would be typical readers, after all), but Cecil had a lot more to say.

Although he said at the end, "On the whole, Lily, you write rather well." That was a big bravo from someone like him. She didn't care for him, but he knew his stuff. She'd have to get down to work. Last week had passed like a couple of days. Writing wasn't fun, but it somehow felt necessary.

5

Cindy looked back at herself sullenly. It was a full-length mirror and revealed thick thighs and a fat butt encased in jeans. It was so annoying when Mom told her what a lovely figure she had; it was just a mother's lie. They always wanted you to eat breakfast and finish your dinner. She'd have to diet more. She already skipped breakfast, taking it with her in the morning, claiming she was late, and dumping it in the first trash can she came across. Lunch was just an apple, but they wouldn't let her cut out dinner. They were clueless, had no idea what she went through with all the popular girls in school allowed out whenever they wanted, allowed to wear as much makeup as they wanted, and some of them looking like real models. All her parents knew was how to be annoying.

When her eight-year-old sister Ellie burst into her room, Cindy turned on her with a snarl. "Don't you ever knock?"

"Sorry Cindy," Ellie said as she retreated. "I only wanted to show you my Christmas dress. How come you're only wearing jeans? It's a party!"

"It's a boring old party I don't want to go to. And I've seen your dress. Now leave me alone! Your squealing gives me a headache."

Cindy turned back to the mirror, and after a couple of minutes, saw her mother's reflection behind hers.

"You'll have to wear something better than that, Cindy. This is Wendy's Christmas party at her house. What about that outfit I got you last month? That would be suitable."

"Mom, it's a heinous outfit. And it doesn't matter what I wear, anyway. I'm too fat to look good in anything. And tell Ellie not to barge into my room like that. She's so annoying."

"Well, sorry we're all so annoying, Cindy, but you *are* to change. We're leaving in twenty minutes. And you are not fat, your weight is perfectly normal. You have a very nice figure."

"Yeah, right."

When her mother had left, Cindy locked the door and took the offending outfit out of the closet. Well, no one she knew or cared about would be there and there'd only be endless fuss if she didn't change. At least it was black, though creepy velvet. Why couldn't they just leave her home? She was sixteen, for God's sake! They were really being stupid about this killer. He only liked little girls. She took her own sweet time to get ready.

The house was a large one for the neighborhood, bigger than those most of Cindy's friends lived in. Lights festooned a fir tree in the front yard, and a holly wreath hung on the door. When Wendy greeted them, Nancy introduced her husband and children. Ellie put on her annoying dimply smile and said, "Hi, how are you? Thank you for having us!"

Wendy, predictably, beamed back and said what a charming and well-mannered little girl Ellie was. Cindy just smiled a little, and said, "How do you do?" She wasn't about to suck up like dumb Ellie. Her father said, "How are you?" in an embarrassingly loud voice as he crushed Wendy's hand in his.

They moved into the living room, a large room that seemed to stretch from the front to the back of the house. The room was already full as they were late, as her mother had harped on about all the way over. Serves them right for messing up her evening and making her wear a cheesy dress. Nancy gave Wendy a Christmas cactus plant and Wendy said she was thrilled it had so many buds on it. Cindy sighed. *These people.*

"Wendy, what a beautiful room, and what marvelously tall windows! You must get lots of light in daytime," said Nancy.

"Yes, I do. As with many of these houses, there were lots of small rooms. This is actually three rooms knocked into one. I use the other end as a dining area and I often sit by the window there where I can look out over the garden."

Cindy wondered if anyone really cared about where Wendy ate and what she looked at while she did it. She noticed a young man sitting near the fire. He caught her eye and got up. He didn't look so bad.

"Hi, I'm Steve. Are you Nancy's kid?"

"Yeah! You're a bit young for this lot, aren't you?"

"Well, I'm twenty now. Older than you, I guess, but I work in the store with your mom. You don't look as if you want to be here."

"No, it's boring."

"They're not all that bad. That's Peter over there. He's the bookkeeper and he never talks to anyone. Always in a bad mood. You've met Wendy. And that's a new person, Lily

Porter. I haven't made her out yet. She's nice, but doesn't give away too much, if you know what I mean. She comes off like she's too good for us sometimes. And that's Mr. Blount. He's teaching writing at the store once a week in the evenings. I personally think Wendy's got the hots for him."

Cindy giggled. "At her age?"

"Oh yeah, you wouldn't believe how the old girls carry on sometimes," said Steve, sniggering and winking.

Cindy began to feel a bit better. Steve wasn't bad looking, and he was still young enough to be cool. Maybe she could get him to go out with her so she could tell her friends she was going out with a twenty-year-old. It might get her into the popular set. She looked around.

"Hey, I thought you said he doesn't talk to anyone," she said, indicating Peter with her chin. Peter was smiling down at Ellie and they were chatting away. God, she could hear the kid's squealy voice from here.

"Weird," said Steve. "He is such a bad-tempered guy; who'd've thought he'd have the patience for a kid."

"Yeah, 'specially her."

"She looks quite a sweet kid."

"Annoying."

"I see. I had one of those once."

"You don't have her anymore?"

"No, she grew up. She's almost normal now."

Nancy came over with Lily and introduced her. Lily asked about Cindy's school, and Nancy answered most of the questions, which made Cindy squirm, and then Nancy and Steve got into a discussion about how best to sort books for shelving. Cindy studied Lily, who was studying everyone else, and realized that Lily didn't feel part of this group either. She was a bit snobbish, she decided. Thought she was better than everyone else. It showed in the way she watched Steve and Nancy, looking down her nose with a grudging smile on her face. Her voice was snobby too, as if she were trying too hard. Lily caught her eye, and it was startling, her expression challenging as if she could read Cindy's mind. Cindy excused herself and walked over to her sister.

"Hello," she said to Peter, ignoring Ellie, of course. He didn't answer, just looked at her as if she were a pile of dog crap and went back to telling Ellie about some stupid teddy bear he'd had once. She shuddered as she thought of his hard gray eyes that hadn't quite met hers, just kind of slid away like water off a windowpane. She went back to Steve. They chatted about music until dinner was ready and they went to fill their plates. Steve said he shared a small apartment with a friend. Better and better! She could cook up a story with Margot, her best friend, and spend some time there. Margot would be impressed for sure and tell everyone else. She asked Steve what he thought about Peter.

"I suppose he's okay. Just gets on with his work. Never says anything. Miserable sort of guy. Don't know anything about him, really. Weird he likes your sister."

"He's creepy. My parents ought to be taking care of Ellie, not letting her bother some stranger."

"Oh, they're just having a good time. They probably don't get out much."

"No, Dad just likes to drink at home and snore in his chair all evening. When they're not having rows, that is."

"Really, your mom doesn't seem like the type for rows. She's really sweet. I like her a lot."

"It's not her, it's him. He doesn't do shit, except drink."

"Poor Nancy. And poor you, I'm sorry."

"Well, at least it keeps him off my back." She took a deep breath. "Hey, you want to catch a movie sometime?"

"I don't know what your mom would have to say about that. Well, I do, actually. She'd say I was too old for you."

"She doesn't have to know, does she?"

"Cindy, I won't go that route. You're a lovely kid. I like you. You're a real looker, too, but I won't upset your mom."

"Okay, I guess," Cindy said.

"Come on, Cindy, let's get dessert. I'm starving."

"Oh, I don't eat much. I'm on a diet."

"Why on earth would a skinny kid like you be on a diet? You'll end up with flat boobs if you lose too much weight, and we wouldn't want that, would we?"

Cindy giggled and went with him to the table. While Cindy was filling her plate, a voice behind her said, "And what's your name?"

She turned and saw the teacher person smiling at her. "I'm Cindy, Nancy's daughter."

"Pleased to meet you. I'm Cecil. I don't know your mother, really, as I'm only at the store on Tuesday evenings. I teach creative writing, you know."

"I'm not very good at writing. Not one of my best subjects."

"Well, I do a lot of tutoring, so if you need any help, just ask your mother to let me know."

"Sure, thanks." Right, like she'd want to go to another stupid class. Although he was kind of cute in a funny sort of way. Nice eyes, nice smile. Those nice eyes looked into hers as if he fancied her or something. *Yuck, too old.* She moved away toward Steve, who was sitting cross-legged at the other end of the room.

Cindy and Steve talked about movies and music, and she tried to watch Cecil out of the corner of her eye to see if he was looking at her. He stared a lot at Peter and Ellie, though. His eyes never left them, and he was smiling as if something amused him. Weird bunch, except for Steve.

"Charades everyone!" said Wendy.

"Oh, God!" moaned Cindy under her breath.

"Come on, we'll have to be good sports," said Steve.

Steve guessed the first one (the name of a quiz show host), and then Cindy had to act out her own clue for her team. It was a hard one (The Tale of Two Cities), but she mimed it well enough for them to get it in record time and was soon laughing like all the rest. It wasn't until Steve nudged her and said, "See, not so bad if you hang loose!" that she realized she'd let herself down and enjoyed herself. She didn't participate again.

Wendy handed out the presents that were under the tree for all the employees and their families and they were unwrapped with cries of delight that were so fake. Most people got books (no surprise there!). Ellie loved her pop-up book of Ottawa (and, of course, squealed very loudly when the parliament building shot up out of the middle pages). Cindy didn't love her so-called classic, *Great Expectations*, which she would never, ever, open. She smirked when she saw that Cecil got a gift, even though he only went in once a week. It was a tie, and he gave Wendy a funny little smile when he thanked her. His face didn't look right for a man who likes a woman, and Cindy felt a bit sorry for Wendy, whom she just knew was going to make a fool of herself. Cecil should have looked at Wendy like he'd looked at Cindy. It didn't seem right for a man of his age to look at her like that. It was uncomfortable to think he liked her. Well, at least she'd found out where Steve lived. Perhaps she could manage to bump into him outside his apartment next week.

When they were leaving, Ellie gave Peter a hug and kiss, which made Cindy want to barf, and gave Wendy one, too, thanking her for a lovely evening. Cindy, minding her manners under her mother's steely eye, shook hands with Wendy and muttered her thanks, said goodbye to Steve more warmly, and turned to find herself face-to-face with Cecil. He took her hand, looked into her eyes, and said goodbye as if she were his girlfriend or something. Cindy blushed and muttered, "Nice to meet you," and almost ran out of the door to catch up with her mother.

Her parents were arguing at the curbside about who was going to drive because her father had had too much to drink as usual. Cindy's stomach clenched. She wished her mother would just let it go, although it was scary when her father drove drunk. Nothing bad ever happened, though, if you didn't count the mangled flowerbeds along the driveway and the missing garage door.

Cindy shoved her way into the front, leaving the back seat to her mother and Ellie. Ellie's excited squealing made Cindy want to strangle her on the way home. Peter said she was really pretty and he really, really loved her red dress. Peter thought that school was very important, but having fun was even more important. Peter was going to take her to the park one day, and she'd get to go on the round-about and the swings. Peter wanted her to draw him a picture of her house. Peter wanted to know about her favorite books and had even read some of them. Peter had had a favorite teddy bear when he was eight, just like her! Cindy was relieved when her father yelled at Ellie to shut up, saving her the trouble. She turned around to glare at Ellie. The kid's chin quivered and her mother put an arm around her and kissed the top of her head. Spoiled brat! Served her right for being so annoying!

Cindy closed her eyes and leaned her head on the window, thinking about Steve. Really cool, not bad. He'd sometimes started to talk like an American gangster when they discussed rock music, and then forgot and acted normal. She didn't think he was really a show-off, though. He'd assured her he didn't usually dress like that, he'd just done it to please Wendy because he knew she didn't like his everyday clothes. She'd get at him somehow. It'd be fantastic to be able to brag to the girls about her boyfriend, who was so much older than them and had a real job, too. She hoped she'd never run into Cecil again. Cecil—what a dumb name.

6

Lily hunched over her new desk, gnawing her thumb and staring out of the window. Hilda hadn't minded her bringing in the desk and chair when Lily joined the writing class. The antique cherry piece went well with the white and rose theme in the room, and she'd bought a lamp with a white silk shade so the light would fall on her books just right. Hilda's pride and joy—the rose pink lampshade over-head—cast too many shadows.

The snow, gentle earlier but driven to madness by the wind now, made Lily glad of the radiator just beside her. So comforting to hear the little thuds of icy snow on the window while basking in shelter and warmth. She'd given ten dollars to an old woman on the street near the book-store yesterday and wondered if she sheltered in a warm place now, or lay freezing to death in some dark doorway. She'd never given money to beggars before, felt they should get a job and make their own way. That was before she read a Toronto Star series about homeless people, some overwhelmed by mental illness, job loss, old age; one young man featured suffered from mental retardation—a boy no one wanted or loved. The city did its best, but money was always tight and some inevitably fell by the wayside. And some refused help, either due to misplaced pride or mental illness.

The story touched her; she and her sister hadn't been wanted or loved by anyone either. Poor old Daisy, hooking at sixteen. Not that she'd had anything to lose—their introduction to sex had been early and ugly. Daisy went on to make quite a good living from hairdressing, not very bright, but she'd done all right. Lily had wanted more, and that had taken enormous reserves of strength. People who got in her way had to be disposed of. Killing wasn't as easy as people thought. And not getting caught was no mean feat, either. She shuddered as she remembered the ghastly game of dominos she'd had to play—killing her friend Judy to keep her quiet, then Gayle because she'd seen her through the shades and blackmailed her, then Samantha to throw the police off course, and so it had gone on. What else could she have done? Perhaps she should have thought it all through more carefully.

The hospital for the criminally insane had been nightmarish. It occurred to her for the first time that prison must have been worse for Dad, especially knowing himself innocent of killing her baby sister. Although, always drunk, maybe he couldn't really remember one way or the other. Had he ever realized she'd framed him? But someone like him had no fine sensibilities, unlike her, so on second thoughts, prison wouldn't have been so bad. Except for being forced to stay sober. They'd killed him, though, didn't like people who hurt children. Good riddance, filthy pervert.

She grinned as she relived her successful masquerade as a paranoid schizophrenic. She could have gone on the stage! It got her out of prison and into that grisly hospital for the criminally insane. And, not being insane, it hadn't been so hard to escape. She was much smarter than most. But fragments and flashes bedeviled her, intruding in unguarded moments. She wasn't a killer by nature, just a woman who'd had to take care of herself. What else could she do? She had to keep asking herself that, reminding herself that she'd had no option.

Could she have managed everything without the killing? Her baby sister was different from all the others. She'd saved her from the horror and degradation of her father's perversion, and her death and their father's imprisonment had granted Daisy and Lily a certain freedom, although not the same kind of freedom as most other people seemed to enjoy. And what would have happened if Judy had lived to tell their friends about her background? She'd heard Judy say about a friend's adopted child who'd turned out badly, "Bad blood will out." She'd winced at that, and held onto it, sealing Judy's fate. Still, Lily could have just walked away and started again. What had been so important about keeping the regard of those self-important upstarts? How different things could have been if she hadn't killed anyone. She'd still have her children, especially Andrew, but she never thought she'd be caught. She'd gone on killing her way out of discovery like a cornered rat until she'd begun to make mistakes. And she shouldn't have tried to kill her friends. Not even malicious old Susan.

And who killed that other woman ... what was her name? Anita something. Susan? The woman had enraged her with her contemptuous confrontation at the symphony's Christmas fundraiser. Susan, always used to browbeating people, had looked incredulous when Anita remained unmoved by the venom directed her way. But Susan? A killer? Did she think it would just get lumped in with the other murders? Well, she'd never know now. She hadn't really known Susan any better than Susan had known her. Maybe that murder had nothing to do with any of them.

None of the papers Lily read while she was in Syracuse had mentioned her journal. They must have found it. Did Andrew know about it? It contained the whole truth. If he knew the whole truth, he might feel better about her. Should she write another journal instead of this silly romance novel? She wanted Andrew to love her still. She wanted that.

Lily lay down on her bed and pressed her palms over her eyes. No, that was all behind her and had to stay behind her. She wasn't going to do such things anymore. Killing was not an option, nor writing about it, not even thinking about it. She got stomachaches now when she thought about killing. Planning a killing used to calm her, but now it would roil her guts. The actual killing part wouldn't come hard. It was the "what ifs" that got to her now, now that she'd been caught once, had a taste of confinement, of not being in control. No more. The end.

Lily sat up. She could peer into the shadows, or she could look out of the window. She got up to go back to her desk. There was a rap on the door, a welcome interruption to her mind's nagging and pulling.

"I know you're busy, dear, but I thought you could do with a nice cup of hot cocoa."

Lily rushed to the door to take it from her. "Oh, Hilda, that is so kind. However did you get up the stairs with it?"

"Well, dear, I have my little ways." Hilda straightened her shoulders and awarded Lily a pursed smile. "The cup's not very full, of course. Horrid weather, isn't it? I suppose you're not used to this kind of a winter." A prim folding of hands.

"Well, yes, I am. Manitoba winters are pretty grim. Although I read in the Star that even there it started a lot later this year than usual. Magaly said you usually get your first snow in October, so we can't complain."

"No, we were lucky this year. Well, I'm off to bed. I had my cocoa downstairs. Sleep tight."

They'd sounded as if they were in a Harold Pinter play. Dull and funny in a comfortable sort of way. Lily could see why people loved this safe way of touching. "Good night, Hilda, and thank you again."

"Don't mention it, dear."

Lily thought again about the old homeless lady she'd given money to. She had looked a little like Hilda. It could have been Hilda, with a bit of bad luck. Her relationship with Magaly and Hilda was quite unlike any other she'd known. She'd been born Pansy, but that girl wouldn't have been good enough for anyone in Salton and had to remain hidden inside a new persona, Rose, who had been just right until she was caught. Lily wasn't being held up to the scrutiny of a social set, although she must still hide her secrets, but for a different reason—killers tend to make people nervous. She wasn't a killer anymore, only a lone woman adrift in a foreign city.

She could afford to bask in the old ladies' affection. And she liked it. They were probably the way mothers and aunts ought to be. In their presence, she could have some of the feelings that other people seemed to have. Several times, she had been moved by their kindness and she actually worried about them if they seemed unwell. She'd only drifted up against people before; she'd been a figment of their perception whilst guarding an impenetrable core. She'd never cared enough to form an intimate friendship—that had to be a two-way street. She'd only filed away interesting, and sometimes useful, observations and gleanings from gossipmongers.

Christmas. They'd started the morning at Hilda's house with tea and coffee in the living room, Lily fetching the gifts from under the tree and reading the tags with dramatic flourishes. The oohs and aahs were sweet as Lily found herself caught up in the spirit. The fuzzy bunny slippers from Hilda warmed her feet now and Magaly's bed jacket was a blessing for reading in bed on these cold winter nights. The ladies had loved the real silk scarves Lily had picked up in a downtown boutique. Neither of them had possessed such a luxury before. And then the three of them getting in each other's way preparing an early dinner. Sherry before dinner and wine with brought high color to their cheeks and much giggling and gossiping. Thank heavens none of their kids had chosen to come. They would have spoiled everything. She'd remember that day for the rest of her life. She'd had many good Christmases with her family, but this one had broken a long drought filled with fear and longing.

Lily looked down at the blank page as she scratched her head with her pen. Cecil had set them an exercise. Pick two characters from your story, one nice and one not so nice, and write descriptions of them. The answers to a list of questions had to be incorporated into the pieces.

"How does he/she feel when looking down on a baby asleep in a crib?" *Melting tenderness*, Lily decided, because she'd read it somewhere. She had no idea what that would feel like beyond a sense of achievement at having produced this little thing and an instinctive protectiveness. Except Andrew: a pleasurable tenderness for him had sometimes taken her unawares. She mustn't think about the children now. Impatient with herself, she crossed out what she had written—she must learn to cut and paste. *Regret,* she wrote, *for all the bad things she couldn't stop happening to this beautiful baby, and for her inevitable loss of innocence as she makes her way through an ugly world.*

Tomorrow, Monday, and a day off. She'd visit the Art Gallery of Ontario again. Her heroine could meet her romantic hero at the restaurant there. Perhaps she—was Eva a better name than Laura?—should work there. She loved the little glass-walled restaurant set up at one end of a sculpture atrium; on a clear day when the winter sun poured through, it was idyllic. After lunch, she'd tour one of the galleries she hadn't seen yet. She didn't like to "do" museums and galleries; she liked to take them slowly, absorb the exhibits, and think about them. If she got an internet account, she could learn more about the artists and their times. She still felt so unsure of the word processing system she wrote first with pencil and paper before typing her work. It would come; she felt more competent every day.

Laura envied her best friend, Karen. Married to a lovely man, mother of a beautiful baby boy. Saturday night, and here she was babysitting while the married couple took in a movie and dinner. Something's wrong with this scenario, she thought. The rocker almost put her to sleep as she soothed the colicky baby. She kissed his warm fuzzy head and smelled the baby powder scent that made it all seem so idyllic until the inevitable arrival of the poop bomb. Oh well, romance and reality would always be at odds. She took him off her shoulder and cradled him in her left arm. A Churchillian face she hoped would become a child's puckish features, then rugged good looks. And what will you do to the girls, little boy? Be nice, be kind, pick them carefully. Very carefully.

Victor had been nice for years. Until he began to love his daughter more than his wife. Until he got sick and his wife remained in above-average good health. Until he got so depressed he made her life a misery. But she released him from all that. Did him a favor. Enough. Drop it, push the past down, way down deep. Bedtime.

Interesting menu again. The current major exhibit this month featured French impressionists of the twentieth century and the café had reflected that in the food selection. She'd have escargots. She remembered her first taste, Victor looking on with amusement—he'd been a doting husband then. And *coq au vin*. Good, she wouldn't bother with dinner.

Lily walked out of the museum, still entranced with Venice. She'd ended up in the collection of Canaletto's views of Venice. She'd love to visit La Serenissima one day. It would be fascinating to see how it looked now, its own hard edges rather than the artist's soft ones, modern life intruding on the old spaces. She imagined the music of the Italian language all around her. She'd once decided to study French, but maybe Italian would be more fun.

She strolled along Dundas and turned onto Spadina in what she thought might be the direction of a convenient street car stop near the University of Toronto. She enjoyed walking in Toronto. Compared to New York, it was clean, green, and many of the buildings were quite fine in a Victorian sort of way. A familiar voice froze her blood. Two men got out of a cab in front of a small restaurant. Toby Elantro, thinner than he used to be, with gray shadows under his eyes, his voice as loud as ever. Lily pulled her hood farther across her face and hurried past, heart and feet pushing at the wind.

She told Hilda she had a headache and would just take a cup of tea up to her room. She couldn't write, although she hadn't finished her character sketches yet. She could hardly find the energy to climb the stairs and her legs felt cold and dead as she dragged herself up to her room, where she huddled shivering under the duvet. What if she were recognized? Her hair was a different color and style, but if someone who knew her looked hard enough, they'd see who she was. Would it never end? She curled up and closed her eyes. Killing Toby's wife was her biggest mistake. He'd been devastated when he lost Samantha, could hardly function. He would relish the chance to see Lily punished again. Perhaps glasses, tinted glasses. Maybe she needed them at her age. And certainly large dark sunglasses while she wandered around Toronto.

The warmth lulled Lily into a fitful sleep until the sound of Samantha's head smashing onto the concrete of the garage floor jolted her awake. She was shaking again, couldn't stop. She remembered Toby's sagging shoulders, voice rasping with grief, and his flight from Salton. Samantha hadn't deserved what happened, and neither had Toby, but Lily had had to cast suspicion away from herself; killing Samantha and making it seem like a suicide had seemed the perfect way to do it. But it hadn't worked, and that had been the beginning of the end for Lily. What a stupid waste. *Stupid, stupid.*

Three a.m. She wouldn't be able to sleep again, so she went to her desk and turned on the lamp. Her writing was shaky, and she had an annoying flicker in her right eyelid, although her headache was better.

Question: *How would he/she feel if caught in a big lie by a friend?* Answer: *Murderous rage and desire for revenge. Would have to make sure the story never got out.* See, that could be considered quite a normal reaction. Lily went back to bed and fell asleep almost immediately.

7

Lily helped Steve sort books for shelving in the back room the next morning, still not feeling quite well and still annoyed by a flickering eyelid. It called attention to her face.

"There are a lot of biographies today, aren't there?" Steve said.

"Yes, they seem very popular now."

"I'd rather read about celebrities than a bunch of dead people. Peter's always reading about dead people. Maybe that's why he's so weird," Steve said.

"Well, reading about the past can help us better see the future. What do you mean, Peter's weird?" She was curious to know what he thought of the man.

"He's weird because he doesn't really look at you properly when he talks, more like he's talking to someone over your shoulder. When he talks to anyone, that is. Actually, you used to do that. Until you got to know us."

"Did I? I didn't realize that." *Cheeky brat.* Did they think her weird?

"And he seems to hate everyone except Nancy's little girl. Did you see them at Wendy's party?" Lily nodded. "And I don't see what anything in the past has got to do with the future."

"You wouldn't at your age. When you get older, you start to see patterns."

"I don't get it."

"You will."

"Well, I'm going to take my break now." He slouched off, too cool for words.

So annoying he never wondered if she'd like to go first. These youngsters, never taught any manners. Interesting he found Peter weird, though. She'd have to pay more attention. She wheeled the cart to the music section and began to shelve, starting with the classical selection. When she moved toward the popular music area, a group of books that Steve had piled there caught her eye. *Beetles Are Everywhere* by Andrew Evans. Little twit!

The store wasn't busy after New Year's, so the staff took it in turns to leave early. Nancy was leaving early today to have dinner out with her husband and younger daughter, Ellie. She had gone home in the middle of the afternoon to get Ellie dressed, and brought her back to the store where her husband was to pick them up.

The little girl looked so pretty in her green velvet dress and patent leather shoes, her gleaming, dark hair held back in a ponytail by a green satin ribbon. She bubbled excitement about going to a real restaurant and her grownup appearance. Her mother looked down at her with fond amusement as she twirled around to make her dress float around her legs. Lily thought of her own daughter at that age, who wouldn't consider wearing anything but jeans unless threatened with grounding. Lucy dressed quite well now. Her eyelid flickered harder. People in control don't twitch. Mustn't think about the children, the past. Set it aside.

"Don't get messy, now. We're going to meet Daddy in an hour and go to dinner together. You'll want to look your best." Nancy smiled and stroked Ellie's hair.

"It's so hard to sit still for a whole hour, Mommy," said the shrill little voice.

"Why don't you come and sit at my desk," Peter offered. "I've got some work to do, and you could draw me a picture of you and your parents in the restaurant."

"But I don't know what the restaurant will be like."

"Just imagine how you would like it to be. Come on, I've got some crayons in my drawer."

Ellie bounded over to his desk and sat opposite him on the visitor's chair, wriggling her bottom into the cushion. He passed over paper and crayons and a candy bar.

"Only one bite, now. Save the rest until after dinner," said Peter sweetly.

"Okay." She smiled like an angel. "Thank you, Peter."

"You're very welcome."

Everyone's head had pivoted Peter's way. He rarely spoke a word to anyone, and only then if it were unavoidable. And here he was, being chatty and kind again with Ellie. Peter looked up at them all defiantly and they turned away, embarrassed by their overt surprise.

Strange that a grown man without children should have crayons in his drawer. Alert suddenly to every nuance—each expression, each gesture, the tone of his words—Lily watched him while she sorted the new books. What seemed merely out of the ordinary to others stank of rottenness to her. Her skin pricked, her eyes, too, and her breath came in spurts.

Peter came around the desk and looked over the child's shoulder as he stroked her hair. He complimented Ellie on her artistry, and when the child turned to look up at him, his eyes locked on hers—the gaze of a man in love. Lily straightened and stared at him, appalled.

Her focus blurred as a knot formed in her stomach and her head began to pound as childhood memories demanded their place. She knew what he was and Peter, turning suddenly to look her way, saw that she knew. His smile tightened into a grimace. Lily summoned a false bright grin and turned back to her task.

The next day, Lily pleaded a headache and left work early. She stopped in a public restroom, donned the garb of a bag lady, then sat in a doorway where she could see the store and wait for Peter to emerge. His chubby figure with its rolling walk soon appeared, and she followed him to a fast-food restaurant where she had to show her money before she could get served, so she must look like the real thing. She followed him to the park, where he sat on a bench by the children's playground. He looked at the children the way most men look at strippers. She felt sick again. He looked toward her.

"Weren't you at Sam's? Are you following me or something?" he accused in a rough voice.

"Why would I follow you? Perhaps you're following me!" she said in a wheedling way she hoped was believable. "I like to watch little kids. And I can tell you do, too. Really."

Peter sprang up and jogged from the playground. Lily went home after another stop to change—she could hardly approach Hilda's house looking like that.

The next morning Wendy greeted her with, "Did you hear the news, Lily? Another little girl taken."

"I'm so scared for my two," said Nancy. "I dare not let them out alone anymore, even though it makes Cindy mad. I know he goes after younger children than her, but you never know."

Lily looked at Peter. He didn't look at anybody and didn't enter the conversation. Lily felt a sort of red light behind her eyes. She took a deep breath. She must get a grip on herself.

During her lunch hour, Lily went to a public phone and called in an anonymous tip with Peter's address. She heard about it on the news that night. The police found nothing and could only apologize and leave. Peter threatened to sue them for destroying his good name, but Lily doubted that he would. He'd just slink back into his slimy existence.

She slept badly that night, troubled by nightmares. Everyone she had ever known pointed an accusing finger at her, condemning her as a whore and killer in a rising cacophony of screeching voices. Her parents' voices were the loudest, their faces contorted with hate. The phone rang, part of the dream at first, until finally awakening her with a start. She ran down the stairs and picked it up, hoping Hilda hadn't heard it. He didn't identify himself, but she knew it was Peter who said, "Mind your own fucking business, lady, or you'll be next." She couldn't answer. The handset fell off the receiver the first time her trembling and sweaty hand tried to hang up. Her cold inner core seemed to have gone missing.

"Wrong number, Hilda," she answered to the fretting inquiry.

Write through it. That was the way to push down that anger, those ruinous thoughts. Write through it.

Laura clutched the seat as the car went careening around another bend in the hills. She hoped Dr. Woodbury knew what he was doing. That little creep Peter had finally told him what he wanted to know, where the janitor, Jim, was hiding the boy. She looked sideways at Dr. Woodbury, frightened by the set of his jaw, the fury in his eyes.

"Dr. Woodbury, we have to tread carefully. If he feels threatened, he may hurt him. Why on earth didn't Peter tell us before? Is he afraid of Jim?"

"Jim's his uncle. Peter is a scholarship boy, or was. We kept the relationship quiet. A lot of the students picked on him, anyway. I think he tried too hard to fit in."

"Yes, he is rather gauche. Do you think his uncle did anything bad to him?"

"Who knows? There will be a full police investigation, believe me."

"Shouldn't the police handle the search? They have more experience."

"Come on, Laura, this is Hicksville you're talking about. Anyway, I told Mrs. Gray to call them. They shouldn't be far behind."

It seemed like an hour before they spotted smoke behind an outcrop. Dr.

Woodbury slowed down and parked on a grassy patch in front of a rockfall. They got out of the car and moved forward quietly.

"Stay behind me, whatever you do," he whispered.

No hope of that, so she didn't reply. The little shack was mostly hidden by a stand of scrubby pines that spread almost as far back as the road. They tiptoed from tree to tree, hoping Jim didn't have a gun and wasn't keeping close watch. Dr. Woodbury motioned her to stay back and ran, bent double, to the corner closest to the front door. The door opened and a seedy little man peered out before moving toward a woodpile close to Laura. Dr. Woodbury had darted around the side of the house, but now he went inside.

Jim took up an axe and swung it with surprising strength for such a slight creature. He split one log, then another. Laura hoped he would stop soon and go back. The axe was a drawback, for sure. Finally, he dropped it and trudged back to the house, cradling a few logs. Laura crept forward and picked it up. It felt so heavy and unwieldy. She wasn't sure if she'd be any use defending anyone with it.

Jim shot out of the front door, screaming obscenities, his arms flailing out of control, just as Dr. Woodbury walked around the side of the house.

"Looking for someone?" he asked.

Jim stopped dead, his face collapsing in on itself. He sank to his knees, buried his face in his hands, and wept. Sirens came close and stopped and Laura heard heavy boots attempting stealth behind her.

She turned around and said, pointing behind her, "He's there. I think the headmaster's got the boy safe."

"Best hand me that axe, ma'am," one of them said.

Jim had not hurt the boy, although he was badly frightened. Dr. Woodbury seemed exhausted and as they drove home, said little. She invited him to come to her place for a simple dinner and then they could spend the evening relaxing. "I'd like that," he said.

Best case scenario. That's what romance novels are all about.

8

Hilda heard her go out. She could tell Lily was tiptoeing, but the old house still protested every step on its rheumatic old stairs. Lily was a lady through and through, but what sort of lady creeps out of the house in the early hours of the morning? And it wasn't the first time.

Hilda felt sufficiently disturbed to get up and make herself a pot of tea, the only thing for an English lady to do when there's trouble. A lady doesn't whine. She straightens her shoulders and sips a restorative cup of tea. She knew Lily to be a lady, for Hilda had been raised as one herself.

She thought fondly of her father, a true English gentleman (who had supervised all the bookkeepers in a manufacturing company), and his refined wife (who, naturally, did not work, but was a devoted housewife and mother). Poor Mummy and Daddy, they'd been so very dismayed when she married a Canadian and moved to the "frozen north," as they put it. They allowed it wasn't quite as bad as marrying an American—Canadians were a little more civilized thanks to longer exposure to British ways—but still a great disappointment. They had never braved the trip to visit her, and she had never had the money to spare to visit them. Of course, she had never encouraged them to visit, because they would have found out that her husband was a construction worker, albeit a foreman, rather than the man of substance she had described.

She'd been a dutiful daughter, writing once a month until they died, and she had kept to their values. Her husband's family had thought her stuck-up and laughed at her airs and graces. She scowled as she remembered the scene when she entered his mother's house through the back door one Christmas morning and overheard them making fun of her. They hadn't even been embarrassed, just smirked at her through the sodden silence. Her husband had not defended her, and when his face set hard, her heart set hard. He remained silent for the rest of the day, and she held her head high and also remained silent. She didn't care; she had her standards. And there had been no need to see anything more of his family after he died at fifty of a stroke that felled him while he ate a corned beef sandwich on the site one fine spring morning. And she had two lovely sons, after all. Her Jonathon in Quebec had beautiful manners, although Jerry sometimes had to be told to mind his. Jerry, a good boy, lived right here in the city and only sometimes took a little too much whiskey. Worrying. Why couldn't he get married and give her some grandchildren? As it was, she rarely saw him, and she couldn't confide in him because he wouldn't see anything wrong with Lily going out in the dead of night. Thank goodness for Magaly. Magaly, a true friend, even if she was a Hungarian, would understand. As soon as the living room clock chimed nine, she'd call her and go over for a chat.

Lily's sneaking about worried Hilda to no end, though. And it wasn't as if Hilda wasn't broad-minded, no. She was ever such an easy person to get along with, as long as you didn't make a mess or a lot of noise. No, there was something wrong. People Lily's age didn't go about meeting men in the middle of the night, did they? So what was she doing? She would have to ask Lily to come into the kitchen for a little chat when she got home. Hilda raised a corner of the heavy curtain and peered out. Still dark and no sign of her. Maybe she should go back to bed and try to catch forty winks. She'd be sure to hear Lily when she unlocked the door.

Hilda sighed as she made her careful trek back upstairs. There was trouble. She could feel it tingling up her spine. She just hoped her nightmares wouldn't come back. Especially the one about the Christmas party where everyone sang carols around the piano, except Hilda, who was standing in the middle of the room while they all pointed at her, grinning as they sang. The carols were the familiar old tunes, but they had curse words and worse, and were all about Hilda. She always woke up panting as they closed in on her. It couldn't be good for her heart.

She'd think about nice things while waiting for sleep. She'd think about the green hills and cow fields where her father used to take her for walks on Sundays, their border collie frolicking ahead before circling back to round them up. They had enjoyed lovely times together on those walks. They'd stop at a country pub and sit in the garden while Daddy enjoyed his pint of pale ale, and she her fizzy orangeade.

Lily walked in the shadow of the walls, trying to be silent as she followed Peter from his house. She flattened into a doorway whenever she heard a car coming, but managed to keep up. He turned right. She approached silently and peeked around the corner. She couldn't see him, so she slid around so she was still close to the wall. As she passed a doorway, she felt the sudden shock of a blow to her temple. The pain spread through her head like a spider's web, and as she fell to the ground, she heard him hiss, "Leave me alone, bitch." Before she passed out, she heard his car hawk and spit as it always did.

She came to and lay there for a few minutes, pressing an icy-hard palm to her head. Pain. Had Samantha felt pain before she died? Her knee hurt and her hands smarted where she'd fallen on them. Nothing else damaged? She got up gingerly and braced herself against the doorway. She breathed the cutting cold air into her lungs and tried to get her bearings. In this arctic weather, she was surprised she could feel anything. *A cab, must find one.* She started to walk and put her thoughts aside for a while so she could concentrate on getting one foot in front of the other. She fingered her wallet, still in her zippered pocket. Lights at last, and people. She had no idea of the time, nor how long she'd been walking. A cinema. And a taxi stand. She heaved herself into the first one.

"Lady, are you drunk? I don't take drunks or crazies."

"No, I was mugged, but they didn't get my wallet, thank heavens."

"Okay, then. Where to?"

Lily poured herself some water, took two aspirins from Hilda's bottle, and went straight to bed. In the morning, she staggered downstairs with a dreadful headache and sat down at the kitchen table. Hilda took a chair opposite and peered into her face. Her bird-bright eyes crinkled at the edges with worry.

"Well, Lily. Just look at those black eyes! You're going to have to tell me what's going on. It's worried me, all your comings and goings at all hours of the night. I have a right to know what's going on!" Her voice warbled as it rose.

Magaly knocked and entered, all in one motion, it seemed.

"My God, Lily. What have we here?" she said, her booming voice making Lily cringe.

"Ladies, I have such a headache." She couldn't hide this anymore. "I'm going to tell you what's going on. But, please, could one of you call Wendy and tell her I can't make it? I don't feel up to it."

"I will do that," said Magaly, and she clomped out to the phone.

Lily heard her declare, "Got a bad, bad headache and sore throat, too. Flu, I think. Be a couple of days at least, I should say."

Magaly came back and planted herself on her chair. "Well, now."

"I need to know what's going on," Hilda said plaintively. "Both of us do."

Lily told them about Ellie's visit to the store, Peter's behavior at the playground, her following Peter to see if she could find out anything, and how he must have spotted her last night and knocked her out.

"I think I was only unconscious for about ten minutes, if that."

"Just as well in this weather," said Magaly, her fists tight. "You could have got dead."

Hilda said nothing. She'd turned pale and her hand trembled as she brought her cup to her lips.

Lily licked her lips. "Hilda, could I possibly have a cup of tea? My mouth is so dry."

Magaly looked at Hilda and got up to pour a cup of coffee for Lily.

"It is coffee you need at a time like this, something strong," she said.

"Nonsense, everybody knows tea's the thing when you're feeling down," protested Hilda, and she got up to put the kettle on.

"Pshaw! Well, drink first the coffee, and then have the tea."

Too tired to argue, Lily sipped the bitter black brew.

"Lily," said Hilda at last. "You must leave things alone. You might get really hurt, or worse. These are matters for the police."

"I called the police, but they didn't find anything."

"There's nothing you can do. Let it be, let it be," pleaded Hilda.

Magaly pursed her lips. "If this man is the monster, he must be caught and punished," she said. "I am for helping you, Lily. I can do some following in daytime. He will never suspect me."

"I couldn't let you run the risk." In truth, Lily felt more than willing to let Magaly take the risk.

"My little sister was killed by one of those fiends. They knew who it was, everyone did. But they couldn't prove anything. Then, when the Russians were coming, we knew that everything would be—how do you say?—Chaos, no more law. So my father and brothers took care of him good. My parents were never the same. It destroyed them, thinking of her, so frightened and hurting. A little bit of all of us died the day they found her. Yes, I do whatever is needed to do. And I am proud of you, Lily, for going after him." Magaly looked like old royalty, the way she sat and surveyed them both.

"Thank you, Magaly." Lily was touched by the old woman's courage.

"Oh dear," Hilda whispered.

Lily went back to bed.

Lily was still home a couple of days after her accident. Hilda had persuaded her to go to the clinic, and the doctor had dressed her wound and prescribed strict bed rest. He told her bluntly that she was a fool not to have gone straight to a hospital in an ambulance after the mugging. Head wounds were not to be trifled with. He'd sounded outraged.

She lay on the sofa in the living room watching the noon news from Buffalo while Hilda was out shopping. The last item winded her. A young attorney had been murdered in California under strange circumstances. His girlfriend was missing and presumed abducted. He had been stabbed, then drowned in a fish pond. The picture was fuzzy, nevertheless he looked just like Andrew. Lily's head spun, and she took little gasps of breath as if her air were rationed. She had missed the name. "Not Andrew, not Andrew, not my son," she muttered over and over. She staggered up the stairs and got under the duvet.

After a while Hilda called up, "Are you all right, dear? Only you left the TV on."

Lily pulled herself together. "Yes, fine, thank you. Sorry I forgot to turn it off. I wasn't feeling well, suddenly. I'm going to take a nap."

As she lay in bed, her thoughts fractured like thin ice. Maybe it wasn't him. But it looked like him and she had no idea where he had moved to after she was convicted. California would make sense, as far away from Salton and Washington, D.C. as possible. She'd watch the evening news at six. She looked at her watch. Five hours from now. She stared at the ceiling, her eyelid winking madly now. Her headache flared up, her stomach ached, her soul ached.

Sukie's face popped into her mind. How she had hated that girl, although she realized too late she should never have killed her. She'd been pretty, too. How had her parents felt? Like this? And what about the boyfriend she'd framed? How would she have felt if Andrew were sent to prison for murder? Especially one he hadn't committed. Lily tried to banish these thoughts from her mind. Not her problem anymore. And there was Gayle. She was young. She must have had parents who loved her. Well, not necessarily; not everyone did. Not Lily, certainly. Why hadn't she ever thought about these things at the time? She'd had no feelings at all then, except when she got those feelings that Peter had reawakened, and she would go home, lie in bed, and plan. Planning the killings had calmed her. And killing had been like an exorcism. She'd sworn she would never kill again, but if it was Andrew, she'd have to avenge him. Have to.

Spent by turmoil, Lily fell asleep.

The six o'clock news reported again on the young attorney's death. They showed a better picture this time, and a name. Not Andrew. Lily rested her head on the back of the wing chair and closed her eyes. She felt weak again. Was she going to have a stomachache for the rest of her life? Hilda called her into the kitchen for dinner.

"I've made you a little poached fish and some baby potatoes. That's easy to digest when you're not feeling well."

"Thank you so much, Hilda, you are kind to me. You must let me know the extra I owe you."

"Not at all, dear, not at all."

She'd buy some groceries when she felt well enough. She knew Hilda had to watch every penny. She forced her dinner down and rose to clear the table. Hilda wouldn't let her.

"Let me finish this, Lily. You don't look well today. I think you should take a nice hot drink to bed. Do you have something nice to read?"

"Yes, and I have homework, too."

"No, no homework tonight, dear. Just a nice rest."

A nice hot drink, a nice book, a nice rest. It was nice being mothered, very nice indeed.

9

P eter slammed his front door behind him before trudging up the stairs to his mother's bedroom. He took a duster out of the dresser and dusted the furniture with a delicate touch and ran his hand over the bedcover, although it hadn't been disturbed since the morning, when he'd performed the same ritual. His mother always seemed present in this house, looking down on him, judging him. He no longer felt her wrath, not since she'd passed on, but he always kept her room just as she liked it in case it was still important to her wherever she roosted. He sat in the rocker next to the bed and closed his eyes, looking for any thread of comfort his mother's spirit might allow him. His loneliness was insupportable sometimes.

Poor Mother had never been the same after she got out of prison; it had sucked all the heart out of her. She'd always been the kind one, always trying to protect him from his father's violent outbursts, to no avail; Peter had to be toughened up. His father must make a man of him. Peter, knowing himself a failure in the manhood department, finally escaped to a small college close to the border, leaving her alone with a brute who had to have someone to turn on in his drunken rages. The neighbors never suspected what went on in this house and so, when she showed the police his bloody corpse, kitchen knife still firmly in place, she'd been charged with murder. She explained how she'd been beaten, but she couldn't prove it as he hadn't started that night, was just about to, and her bruises had faded since the last time. No one knew any different, except Peter. No one took any notice of a boy trying to save his mother.

He remembered his excitement the day Mother came home. He'd cleaned and cooked and put up a "Welcome Home" sign. But she'd become arthritic and sour, terminally broken. She'd demanded and complained, developed asthma and diabetes, then cancer, and had taken her own sweet time dying. He'd finally helped her along with a soft pillow, and no one thought to check.

He couldn't bear to watch her suffering, to listen to that high querulous voice and heed the persistent ring of her bell, which called him to her side with imperious immediacy, day and night—he still heard it sometimes, waking in the dead of night and half out of bed until he remembered. He'd stopped looking with love upon the parchment-covered skull with its obscene slash of bright lipstick, which he, unwilling and repulsed, was directed to paint on each morning. She'd been china doll pretty when she was younger, and when his father was out at work, she'd entice him into her bed for a cuddle. They had no one else; they needed the comfort. Peter drew back the coverlet, climbed carefully onto the bed, and buried his face in the pillows, remembering.

Just after he turned fourteen, he'd noticed a quickening in his groin one afternoon, and she noticed, too. He'd felt confused and embarrassed, and dirty, too. She told him it was quite normal and he should learn all about these things. He hadn't known what to think at first. People did those things with girlfriends and wives, he'd thought. But he'd been lulled into accepting her assurances, and had come to love his mother in quite a different way, and it made him want to kill his father much more than the beatings ever had. On weekends, when his father was home, he suffered the agony of unfulfilled desire, not to mention the sounds of his father's rutting, until Monday afternoon rolled around. His quick fix was to concentrate his mind on homework, so he'd ended up doing quite well. By Sunday night he had to relieve himself in the bathroom, quickly as they only had the one, and no one must know. He'd appreciated the contrast between self-stimulation that brought mere relief, and the soft warmth of his mother's pliant body and their loving intimacy.

While Mother had been in prison, he'd had a few girl-friends, but they were so free and easy, so sure of them-selves, it put him off enough that he didn't even try to make love to them. Mother had been comfortable. She loved him unconditionally and never criticized him, which is why her changed demeanor came as such an unbearable shock. He told her about his dates on one of his Sunday visits, and she told him not to bother with those loose girls; just wait for Mother. He'd be happier in the end. She'd been quite testy, in fact, and he'd had to promise to save himself for her.

He tried once more, though, determined to have sex but, racked with guilt, couldn't. The bitch laughed at him and he just knew she'd told her friends. Never again, he swore, Mother was right. When she came home, she still liked their cuddles, but wasn't much interested in anything else. Her health, he supposed, but he'd suffered at first. And when she got really bad, it was out of the question, and she got god-awful ugly, too; even the thought of touching her to take care of her needs started to make him feel sick. She'd ruined him for normal love, but Dad had ruined her. Everyone ruined everyone. Nevertheless, after she died, he'd grieved and sobbed for her for two solid years. Then he had to get on with life. A life he was determined not to spend alone.

He'd had to get a job, for one thing. Their savings were running low and her social services checks had stopped coming. He'd enjoyed working as a bookkeeper before Mother came home, so took the job at Wendy's Words. He liked reading. It was all he did when he was home, except for taking care of the house. He didn't like anyone at work very much. They were all infuriating nitwits. His nerves frayed as time went on and any frustration could set him on the verge of exploding with rage. But he had to keep his head down and swallow it. He needed the job and could walk from home. He only kept his old car for special occasions and bad weather. He'd heard them in the store making fun of the strange noises it made. Well, walking home for lunch suited him better because he didn't have to endure anyone's company while he ate. Plus, he could let loose if he felt like it, could berate the empty house as much and as loudly as he wanted. He frightened himself sometimes. Perhaps he was becoming his father, spinning out of control.

On one of his rare outings to Eaton's, he found himself standing next to a young woman and her daughter. They were choosing a birthday gift for the girl to give her father. The child was pretty and delicate, sweet, charming, and beautifully dressed. He moved away when he noticed the mother frowning at him, realizing that he'd been staring at her daughter for too long. He spent the rest of the day in a dream, which developed into a plan.

The first girl had been a bungled operation. He'd brought her here, to Mother's room. Perhaps that's why it hadn't worked. Mother hadn't liked him using her room and planted ideas in the child's head. He'd bought toys that were too babyish and pretty clothes that were too big. He hadn't tied her up tightly enough, so when he came home for lunch, he saw her banging on the window and screaming. He'd tried to explain how he just wanted her to be happy here with him, how they'd get married when she was old enough, how they'd go to a new place and be together always. She'd gone berserk then, screeching and crying, and shouting she wanted to go home, not be with an old freak like him. He lost it and hit her. After that, he knew she'd never come to love him and he'd have to get rid of her. It was harder than he'd expected, but when he thought back on it later, quite exciting, had made him feel strangely light. There was a place where he used to sometimes go and hide for hours when his father was on one of his rampages. It wasn't too far, near the lake, with lots of trees and bushes. He rolled her in a blanket and carried her to the trunk of his car. He'd rolled her out of the blanket, which he'd thrown on a sleeping drunk in an alley halfway home. That part of it had gone off without a hitch.

He planned better for the next one. He rented a storage unit and fixed it up with some cheap furniture. The girl should be younger this time. The first had been eleven. Eight or nine would be better, easier to control. It didn't take long to spot a good candidate. She had a babysitter after school who let her go to the playground down the street on her own. He pulled up next to her just before she got home; it was almost dark, perfect timing. There was no one around and she fell for the lost dog routine. But she wouldn't settle down either, and he couldn't stand the racket. Her mother went out to work each day and left her, so they couldn't have been that important to each other. All he wanted was a special friend. He'd wait for sex until she was old enough. He wasn't a freak, like the first one said. And she'd had such a lovely mass of dark curls.

He realized now that he'd have to be patient, have to keep trying until the right girl came along. The kind of girl he could fashion into his special friend for life, his wife. You couldn't trust women, and they didn't like him because he didn't know how to act around them. No, he'd have to get one he could train up.

Ellie, now, she might work out. She was a lovely little girl and smart, too. But that Lily, she was suspicious of him and had followed him last night. She wasn't very subtle, and he'd taught her a lesson, he hoped. She'd watched him talk to Ellie and understood he liked Ellie in a special way. But not in the way she thought; she couldn't know his long-term plan. The police had been around after the last girl was found and he was sure she'd been the one to call in the tip. They'd found nothing, of course. He was too smart for that. And now there was another girl missing, but that had nothing to do with him. She was fifteen, too old for him. They were just assuming, people always assumed things, and they always got it wrong.

The woman in the playground. He'd been watching the girls, looking for a good one, when he'd caught her staring at him. Could that have been Lily? The voice had sounded wrong for a bag lady. She'd have to be dealt with. He couldn't risk her interfering. He had to have the path clear to Ellie. She might be the one.

The doorbell jolted him out of his reverie. He ignored it, but whoever it was kept ringing and knocking. He got up and smoothed down the bed before going downstairs. He opened the door a crack.

"Hello, Peter. Just thought I'd pay a visit."

"Cecil! How did you know where I live?"

"The phone book. Aren't you going to ask me in?"

"Well, it's not convenient right now."

"I bet you don't have plans, Peter. And I want to discuss a couple of girls we both know."

"What do you mean? I'm not interested." Peter felt rage boiling up. He swallowed and almost retched.

"Oh, I think you are." Cecil pushed past Peter and sauntered through to the kitchen.

He sat himself down and looked at Peter with an annoying smirk.

"What do you want, Cecil?"

"I want Cindy. Ellie's sister. Cute kid, sexy. And you want Ellie, I could tell."

"I don't know what you're talking about."

"Okay, go on with your game. I was there in the shop looking for some books for my classes when she came in. I saw you. So did Lily. I saw her face; she picked up on it at once."

"I don't molest little girls. I'd like them to grow up to be someone I would like to be with. There's a difference."

"Don't give me that, the last kid was raped. Don't tell me that wasn't you."

"No, actually, it wasn't me. Not at all. I don't do that."

"What do you do, Peter?"

"Nothing. Nothing that's any of your business."

"Here's my thought. Once Ellie has gone, the parents will be too frantic to pay attention to Cindy. Cindy will need a comforting father figure to turn to. Me. Got it?"

Peter said nothing. Cecil's smirk was hateful. So sure of himself.

"I'm sure you have some little keepsakes from these beauties. Get someone else blamed for it, plant one on someone else, and throw them off the scent. That dumb kid Steve, for example. He'd be the perfect patsy."

Peter looked at Cecil with what he hoped was a blank face. He couldn't risk saying anything. It could be a trap. Cecil was a little rat.

"Well, I'll be off. Think about what I said."

Peter went back upstairs to the rocker. Planting evidence on Steve was an interesting idea. But if he did that, and if Ellie disappeared, he'd be confirming Cecil's suspicions. Maybe the Cindy story was a device to trap him. Maybe Cecil actually liked Ellie. Now that was a possibility. But he'd noticed Lily's reaction, too. He'd have to think. And he'd have to deal with Lily, once and for all. And he should bide his time, let them all think it was over. Lie low. Ellie would still be cute next year.

10

Hilda and Lily perched on opposite sides of the kitchen table, a place where all their important discussions seemed to take place. Lily studied the blemishes in the old painted pine. She felt bereft, somehow, like a child who had been given a pretty doll only to have it snatched back the next day. She was aware of Hilda's bright eyes on her, could feel them, feel their questions. She forced herself to meet their gaze.

"I'm very happy for you, Hilda. I know it will be so much easier for you and Magaly to live in a condo, especially in these awful winters. I will miss you both, though. I can't deny that." She dropped her eyes again.

Miss someone? What was happening to her? What door inside her had opened and let these women in? It felt safe and comfortable, but it couldn't be safe. People could be dangerous. Magaly now, she knew things. She knew there was something about Lily. It was in her tone, in the inclination of her head when she made a comment that was really a question.

"What will you do, Lily? We both have to sell our houses. Where will you go?"

"I'll find a place, perhaps in a house like yours."

"You will visit us, won't you? You know how fond we've become of you."

Yes, she'd visit. She hoped they'd keep enough of Hilda's things to make their condo a cozy haven like this house had become. In her old life, furnishings were born of acquired good taste with all its harmonies, and desire for social status most of all. Now she needed her new place to be cozy in some way. Warm colors, a few antiques, no hard edges. Her own hard edges were eroding, little by little, cup of tea by cup of tea. She felt the sting of tears. The sting of self-disgust. She forced it all away.

"Have you worked out how you're going to do this?" she asked Hilda. "Have you chosen an agent?"

"Jerry said he has a friend in the business. But I don't know."

"Hilda, choose someone who has experience. Talk to several agents. Would you like my help?"

"That would be a relief. Perhaps we can talk to them with Magaly and both have the same agent. But I don't want to upset Jerry."

"Hilda. Do things usually work out with Jerry? Do his ideas ever go well for you? Does he always keep his promises? I don't mean to be unkind, but this is a lot of money we're talking about. You must have a good professional on the job."

It was Hilda's turn to feel the tears now. And she let them spill, let them wend their way through the crannies of her face. She put her pride on hold and let her body slump as she acknowledged her disappointment in his spineless existence, the dashing of her hopes for a son to make her proud, a son who loved her—or anyone else, for that matter. Jerry would never measure up. Lily watched this letting go and ached for her.

"My Jonathon's a good boy, though. Lovely manners. But he's not here, is he? Quebec's a long way away." She dabbed at her eyes. Lily had never known anyone who used little embroidered handkerchiefs before, and she was still fascinated by the delicate wrist turning and pecking as the crumpled silky scrap performed its function.

"No, Hilda, he isn't here. But you have me. I'll look out for your interests. And Magaly's, if she wants me to."

"I should have had a daughter. They stick to their mothers. A daughter like you, Lily, now that would have been nice."

No, it wouldn't have worked out so well. On the other hand, with Hilda for a mother, those imps might not have found entry, would not have stayed lurking in their dark corners, waiting to pull her under. She might have turned out a nice person, a good person. Not as intelligent, perhaps. A boring person, probably. Well, she wouldn't have been her, would she?

Why had Jerry turned out to be such a cad? And as for Jonathon, Lily couldn't remember Hilda ever talking about getting a phone call from him. She would have rushed to tell Lily if she had, all excited and fluttery with her news. There had been a Christmas card, signed "Jonathon." Nothing more.

Lily hadn't learned anything solid about the boys' father from Hilda, but Magaly dropped a few hints now and then. Crude and rude, she gathered, with a family to match. Jerry perhaps took after his father and never considered his mother as an example.

Lily had never looked at her own mother with anything but contempt. She had been the slatternly adjunct to an abusive alcoholic husband who despised her as "common." A stronger character would have left—or made him leave—and acknowledged his abuse of her daughters, soothed their pain, never let it go so far.

Hilda's husband would have treated her with contempt. That's what led the children to be so dismissive. But Hilda wasn't weak. She was proud, too proud to let them see that she minded, would have appeared to be above it all. Showing her unhappiness would have been the weakness in her view. All guesswork, but Lily could see it.

"Lily, are you all right?"

"Oh, sorry, just thinking. Yes, I'm fine. Don't you worry about me. I always fall on my feet. I've got a little homework to do, so I'll be off upstairs. Let me know what Magaly says."

Hilda watched her go, the rigid stance back in place, the face again blank. She worried about that woman. She wasn't quite right. Crushing loss and deep sorrow, Hilda could almost smell it. Oh, she was getting too fanciful, none of her business.

Lily, a strong woman, would act in Hilda's best interests. And Magaly's. She could climb mountains, that one, stare anyone down. Selling the house had seemed like an enormous and daunting enterprise. Lily would take it in her stride, look after it all. Hilda's mind could rest easy now. When you get old, children are supposed to take care of you. Hers would never give her that comfort. She'd brought them up without much sentiment, taught them that one must just get out and on with life. And they had, without looking back. They dismissed her almost as readily as they'd dismissed their father. She'd missed the turn somewhere.

Would she ever learn the whole truth about Lily?

11

The voices in the kitchen rose a few decibels. It was nice having the two old birds together, but it could be wearing sometimes. They bickered a lot, although they never held a grudge. Lily went to the top of the stairs to listen.

"Magaly, why can't you understand how much some of these things mean to me?"

"Hilda, why do they mean so much? All that stuff is in the past and not all of it was good, I think. Do you believe this stuff will mean something to your children? What we should keep is what is nicest. And my sideboard is nicest, for sure. Bela bought it from an old Hungarian fellow downtown. It is right from my country, and heavy. It would be very expensive to buy such a piece now."

"Oh, I don't know. Well," Hilda whined, "kindly tell me what you will allow me to keep. What is good enough for you?"

"Hilda, Hilda, you have a lot of nice stuff. I am not saying you do not. But let us pick the nicest of everything. Let us have a beautiful home."

"All right. But, Magaly, I want my lamps. And my armchair. It's just right for me."

"Yes, but all of the lamps?"

"Yes, all the lamps, all of them." Hilda's voice reached a fever pitch.

Lily decided she'd better go down and create a diversion. And she had a good one. When she went into the living room and sat down, a hundred ancient wrinkles, panicked by the shedding of their lives' markers, turned to her for judgment.

"Hilda, I have found an apartment. It's on this street and quite charming. It's in a house very much like this one. But I need furniture. May I buy some of yours? The things you're not going to need when you move? I'd love to keep my bedroom furniture."

"Even the pink silk lampshade?" asked Hilda plaintively.

"Oh, I know how proud you are of that. I can easily find another."

"What a splendid idea you have, Lily. Doesn't she, Hilda? And we'll be visiting her, so you will still see your stuff."

"Well, yes, that would be a help. Thank you, Lily. We'll have to decide. What do you need?"

"Besides the bedroom, kitchen stuff. Not the table, it's a tiny kitchen. A sofa, a coffee table, a chair or two. Actually, maybe the kitchen table would do for my dining area. A few lamps. Of course, your furniture hasn't been moved out yet, has it, Magaly?"

"No, not for two weeks. Everything else is packed up tidy."

"Okay. If Hilda hasn't got enough left, I could use a few pieces of yours. How about if I hire a couple of fellows to move things around before your final move? Magaly's stuff that's going to the apartment comes over to this house, Hilda. They take the stuff I want to my new place. Anything neither of you wants to keep goes to Magaly's house. And then we can have a sale at Magaly's house to get rid of it. All we need to do is put a notice in the paper."

"That's quite a good idea," said Hilda, relieved someone was making strong decisions.

"All right," Lily said. "Let's make a list."

12

Lily lay back on her bed, tired out. The bare light bulb was irritating. She really must get a lampshade. A soft pink one like Hilda's would be soothing. It had been a difficult ten days. Magaly and Hilda were exhausted and nervous, but they had finally finished with the furniture decisions. The sale had gone well, and they'd given Lily the few little pieces left. Magaly's house had been sold for a decent price and the people would move in soon, just after the old ladies moved to their new home in a couple of days. Hilda was fretting because her house had not yet sold. Lily had soothed her by saying that there had been so much stuffed into it that people couldn't really see its potential—probably the truth.

Lily hadn't met any of the other renters in her new house yet. It was very quiet for the most part. That was what she'd wanted. Quiet and anonymity. But it wasn't very quiet just now. She could hear a cartoon tape playing next door—the

TV seemed to be right up against her bedroom wall. Now the kid was screaming and banging on the floor; it sounded like an out-and-out temper tantrum. Didn't the brat ever go to bed?

The tape was switched off, and the screaming faded as someone dragged the child off to his bedroom. But Lily still couldn't settle. She picked up one of the Agatha Christie mysteries on her nightstand. They were easy to read and evoked an England her father had liked to talk about in the maudlin stage of drunkenness. He liked to give the impression that a classy social set had been his milieu, although the things he let drop at other times contradicted that romantic dream. Lily hadn't been to England, but from other things she'd read, that England was gone forever, and it had certainly never been her father's spot. Hilda seemed to pine for the old England, too. She'd probably be devastated by what she found if she went back, not only because things would be different now, but because it might dawn on her that her memories had transmuted into fantasy over the years.

She missed Hilda and Magaly. And she missed Hilda's house. She hadn't missed anyone before, except her children, especially Andrew. Lily sat up. She had plenty of money. Why didn't she buy the house? She hadn't thought of burdening herself with a house since her escape. But now she wanted it.

Would paying cash attract the wrong sort of attention? She couldn't run the risk of getting a mortgage; they'd find she had no credit history. No, she had told them she'd sold her farm in Manitoba. That's where the money had come from. She'd call the agent tomorrow. She'd better take a look at Hilda's contract. Maybe it had a clause that allowed Hilda to find a buyer, in which case she wouldn't have to pay a commission.

Lily pulled the duvet up to her chin. She'd be able to sleep now. Too bad she wasted the time and money moving to this dump. And let so much furniture slip out of her hands.

"Oh, Lily, Lily, how wonderful!" cried Hilda with tears in her eyes.

"Hilda, I'm only sorry I didn't think of it earlier and save us all this trouble."

"Lily, I won't feel I've lost my house if you've got it!"

Hilda was pink and frothy, elated by being able to hold onto her home in a way altogether satisfactory.

"I'll pay you your asking price, and you'll save on the commission if I read your contract right. The agent won't be happy, but there it is. I've already made an appointment with a lawyer day after tomorrow. He can draw everything up and we'll be on our way to a grand finale!"

"Oh dear me," was all Hilda could manage.

Magaly had not spoken and Lily saw she was close to tears.

"It is a little bit of us that is going to be kept in a good way, Lily. Yes, in a very good way."

Lily felt close to tears herself.

Lily finished packing her things, a very tedious chore to do all over again after such a short time, but at least she hadn't thrown away the boxes. Her angry landlord said he'd keep the security deposit. She told him she had the number of the appropriate complaints department, so he'd better be on solid ground. That shut him up, although he was entitled to compensation, to be fair.

She finished her cocoa and switched off the lamp. Well, she was going to be a homeowner again. Very different this time. A modest little house, nothing fancy. A real home, though. And a pair of old aunts to invite for tea. She almost felt happy.

She woke suddenly, aware of an alien scent. She thought it was a dream at first, but it didn't go away. What was that rustling sound outside her bedroom door? An intruder. She pushed the covers back, swung her feet to the floor, and crept to the door. She peeked around the edge, hoping she wouldn't be seen. The smell was stronger here.

She caught sight of his back through the flames as he rushed out of the house, expelling little yelps with each breath and shaking his right hand as he went. The flames roared in her face. Who always wore that cologne? Shock rendered her amnesiac. Then the searing pain took over as she fought the fire that clutched at her clothes and hair. She smelled her hands and fingers singe as she slapped the orange flames that battled to consume her. Her mind slipped out and up, watching dispassionately as she fought on. Somehow she quenched most of the fire on her body, but the flames had now taken hold of the bedclothes and mattress. She stumbled blindly around the apartment until she found the bathroom and stood under the cold shower, her mind back down in her body now, screaming in an agony too great to comprehend or utter. She slid to the bottom of the tub and panted and moaned while she fought for consciousness—she must try to get out. Stirred by banging on the door, she found herself voiceless. She slipped back into her pain and had retreated too far to acknowledge the paramedics who spoke to her and tried to comfort her, although she knew of them on some level. She was wrapped and moved, which evoked an anguish that drove her mind into its furthermost hole, where it would remain until it felt safe to surface.

Her next concrete memory was of waking in the hospital when a young doctor examined her burns. Pain was present, although the sluggish state of her mind told her that powerful painkillers had rendered it as strident background music. The voice of a young woman came through from her left side. She tried to turn her head, but found she'd been bandaged like an Egyptian mummy and couldn't move.

"I am a police officer. Can you hear me?"

"Yes," she croaked.

"What is your name?"

"Pa… Pa… Lily, Lily Po'er."

"Who did this to you? Someone saw a man running from the house and we know the fire was set. Who was it?"

She scrambled through her addled brain, trying to sort out her thoughts, the simple truths and the unspeakable, and assemble them into the right theme. She was too tired, it was too hard, she didn't want to think. She needed time. She closed her eyes and pretended to sleep.

"It's too soon. You'll have to wait until she can make it on lighter doses. Burn pain is indescribably bad, you know," said a man, probably a doctor.

"I believe it," said the officer. "Even the small burns are bad enough. I can't imagine what a big burn would feel like."

"You don't want to know."

Lily woke later and remembered the police officer after a few minutes. She wanted water and croaked, "Wa'er."

A nurse put a few drops on her lips. "You can't have water, that's why you have a drip."

All Lily could think about was water. She couldn't speak, let alone yell. Thirst consumed her thoughts and took her mind off the lurking agony.

"Do you remember who did this? The police want to know, try to think," said the nurse. "Whenever you can remember and talk, I can get one of them in. And what's your last name? We had trouble understanding you."

Lily didn't answer, but it reminded her she must try to think. It had been her apartment, after all. How could they know who did what? She could implicate Peter and ruin his life. She had tried and failed to expose him, but he could pay for what he had done as a convicted arsonist instead. That would be the easy solution, but his crimes were much worse than that, and he must pay a heavy price. Supposing they found out about her, though—she couldn't give them any reason to probe into her background, because they wouldn't be able to find one.

The young resident, accompanied by a specialist, arrived. The older man looked down at her with as much sympathy as an experienced physician could allow himself.

"Hello, Lily. The apartment and the whole house were too badly burned for the police to find anything out about you. Is there anyone we can call?"

"Work. Bookstore on St. Clair. Wendy's Words."

"Okay. Any family?"

"No one."

"We'll let them know," he said.

"Thanks," she managed.

"We're going to get you well again. Most of your burns were first-degree, except for a few spots on your face and one on your left arm. You've lost the tip of your nose, I'm afraid. You'll need some cosmetic surgery on your face later, but we can make you look pretty good, although different— your friends may not recognize you. You'll never have fingerprints again, so you can take up a life of crime if you like!" He smiled down at her in a clumsy effort at jocularity, but his expression sobered as he registered the gleam that lit up her formerly deadened eyes. She stretched her flame-cracked lips in the semblance of a grin.

She closed her eyes. This agony was worth it, then. She could start all over again, yet again, and go where she liked. She'd stay in Toronto for the time being, but she'd find her children—Andrew, at least. Perhaps she had grandchildren by now. It had been three years since her incarceration in that hellhole loony bin. But she would just be a friend, would never reveal her true identity.

In truth, nobody had ever known who she was, had they? Even she wasn't sure anymore. She had plenty of time to think about which person she had liked the best, which parts of which had felt most comfortable. She could try them all on in her head; she had plenty of time. So far, Lily was the nicest and most comfortable, but she'd worry about all that later. And she had to consider Peter. She had business with him, the serious business of putting a child molester out of commission. Forever, and with as much pain as possible.

She wondered how long she'd be unable to move around, how much longer Peter would be free to find more victims. And Ellie, what of Ellie?

Nothing she could do now. She could work on her story inside her head. For now, she had to sleep. She couldn't help sinking down into that soft cloud.

Laura luxuriated in her warm bed as she revisited her dream. She'd found herself dancing with Gary at the school Christmas party. She remembered wondering how they got there. Gary was a great dancer, had a smile on his face, and was humming "Let's Do It My Way," although that wasn't the tune they were dancing to. He looked downright joyful. Laura danced along clumsily although she'd always considered herself pretty good. But he seemed to almost float above the floor and she couldn't get her footing. She gazed into his face, watching him laugh with excitement and noting a wicked gleam in his eyes she'd never seen before. It was a revelation to see him happy and carefree.

They danced to the next tune, and then the next, getting lighter and happier by the minute, moving faster and faster until they were dancing double-time to the music and whirling around in a dizzying display of virtuosity. The Christmas decorations around the dance floor were the gold and red twirling ones her mother used to hang above the fireplace at home and they bounced before her eyes in what should have been a sickening, disorienting fashion. But it wasn't, it was sheer fantasy and they were young and happy, dancing in fairyland.

Laura stopped focusing on Gary's face and thought only of her own unfettered joy. They didn't stop dancing all night, and the other guests gradually fell away and stood watching them with looks of wonder on their faces, as if they had seen a vision.

When Lily woke she remembered the dream, remembered an earlier very similar one. She wasn't sure if this fit into her novel. Too fantastical? Maybe. Too much Rose's story? Definitely. She must watch out for that. Her journal had recorded it all. It may have been a mistake to leave it for all to see. Had Andrew read it? Did he understand her all the better for it?

13

"Hurry up, Hilda. Lily will be waiting for us."

"I'm coming, I'm coming, it's only just gone eleven."

Magaly toe-tapped and sighed. Hilda fussed so. She always had to find just the right hat, always had to wear gloves, even in warm weather. And the hankies! God, those hankies with their little blue forget-me-knots. These Englishwomen, were they all like that, or had Hilda got stuck in the myths of old England? Magaly had had an English lodger once—ah, so deliciously handsome!—and not at all prim and proper, not at all. In fact… *Now stop that, you are too old for such memories.* Magaly felt her cheeks flush and her stomach tighten as she closed her eyes, ignoring her own admonishment.

"Magaly, are you all right?" Hilda's anxious query broke the moment.

"Yes, of course." Magaly bit her lip, painfully. "Let us get a move on. The bus is coming in five minutes."

The two women got off the elevator and walked the short distance from their building to the bus stop, Hilda with the stiff waddle of arthritic degeneration and Magaly pulling well ahead with her peasant's stride. Hilda made it just as the bus pulled up. A "Heave-ho!" and a good push from Magaly got Hilda aboard in flustered self-consciousness and in a seat near the door.

"Magaly, can't you ever help me quietly? Everybody's staring. They're laughing at me." Hilda's puckered face looked ready for a good cry.

"Do not be so silly. Look, no one is staring, no one cares. This is a city, not a village." She patted Hilda's hand to take the sting out of her words. "I wonder what Lily has prepared for our lunch. She has become quite a good cook, and she has been trying many new things with all this time she has on her hands."

"She's awfully plucky, isn't she? I do admire her so. I can't believe a whole year has gone by since that terrible fire. And she's going back to work soon, too. I wish she didn't have to have any more of those horrid operations."

"Well, only one more on her nose, and not for a few months or so. She looks quite different. And not so bad either, not so bad."

"No, you're right. She looks quite pretty. You have to get up very close to see the scars, especially when she powders the shiny bits."

Magaly leaned back and looked out of the window. In some ways, she missed those weeks they spent in Hilda's old house taking care of Lily while she convalesced. Whenever she got tired of Hilda's fussing, all she had to do was take the bus and come back to their own apartment where she could do whatever she wanted whenever she wanted for a couple of days. Living with another person took some getting used to. Still, Hilda was clean and tidy, and a good person besides. And what of Lily? Did she miss them? Magaly thought so. She sometimes caught a look as they left after a visit, wistful, like a child who had opened her last birthday gift. They had mothered her a great deal, had shown her a lot of love, and she was clearly not used to it; she looked surprised too often.

"I wonder who did that to Lily. Was it meant for her, or did he think someone else lived there? She'd only just moved in, don't forget. I just can't stop wondering."

Hilda said that at least once a week, and Magaly found it tiresome, so she didn't answer, even when she heard her friend's offended puff. She could picture Hilda's look—the pursed lips that deepened the lines around her mouth, the mild frown, the pink spots on her cheekbones. She smiled and relented.

"I am sorry, Hilda. I was miles away. Yes, I wonder too. And, you know, I am sure Lily knows. There was something about her manner when the subject came up after she got home from the hospital. She is hiding something, that one. She knows, I know she knows."

"Magaly, why didn't you say so before? Are you sure? Why doesn't she tell us, or at least the police?" Hilda's voice came out half whisper and half-squeak, discretion warring with indignation.

"I will find the right moment. I believe she is waiting to take her own revenge. I think I know the one she suspects. It is that Peter, that monster. She got too close. You must have thought of it."

"No, I never thought. Oh dear, oh dear, such terrible goings-on! But there haven't been any other killings since then. Perhaps he learned his lesson."

"Hmm." Just waiting for things to quiet down, most likely, but Magaly didn't want to get Hilda riled up again, so kept silent.

The bus stopped close to Lily's house. Hilda didn't find getting off any easier than getting on, and it took both the driver and Magaly to accomplish their descent without catastrophe.

"Oh my goodness, I could certainly do with a cuppa after all that. So exhausting," Hilda panted.

"As you say, exhausting, and I could do with something stronger," Magaly muttered.

"Hello, you two! Come on in." Lily stood at the front gate in gray slacks and a loose cotton sweater of some indeterminate shade of green. She looked dusty.

"You look so well," Hilda said softly as she brushed at Lily with the palm of her hand.

"Yes, sorry, I've been weeding. This warm spell got me thinking about Hilda's lovely daffodils."

"Oh, Lily, I'm so glad you will bring my garden back to life. Did you meet the people who bought Magaly's house yet?"

"No, not yet. They keep to themselves. As do I."

"You should start making some friends, Lily. It will be good for you," Magaly said. "We all need friends, and especially when someone means us harm."

Hilda peered from one to the other. "Magaly is quite right, I'm afraid."

"Where are my manners? Come on in. Lunch is nearly ready. I've made lasagna from a recipe I found in that wonderful cookbook Magaly gave me."

"I didn't know you gave Lily a cookbook, Magaly. You never said."

"Oh, I suppose I forgot. Let us sit down, Hilda, and catch our breath." Magaly fell heavily into one of her old plush armchairs and let out a sigh of pleasure as Hilda selected a new chintz-covered recliner. Lily showed her how to use it, insisting on her putting her feet up against feeble protestations. Magaly wondered if Hilda noticed how deftly Lily had changed the subject. She accepted the glass of sherry Lily offered and listened, half amused and half irritated, as Hilda quibbled about whether or not she should drink in the middle of the day. "Just take it, Hilda, you always do, and you always enjoy it," Magaly said. Hilda frowned and subsided, her cheeks pink again. Lily sighed. Hilda's dithering was getting worse. Must be old age.

"Well, I go back to work tomorrow. I'm really looking forward to it, I can tell you," Lily said as she sat in Hilda's old rocking chair.

"Oh, are you sure it's not too soon? And won't *he* be there?"

"Whoever do you mean, Hilda?" Lily's voice had turned cold.

"Well, you know..."

Magaly came to the rescue. "She means Peter, Lily. He was the one who set your apartment on fire, wasn't he? Who else would want to do that? You said you saw a man running away. You recognized him, I think. You did." Magaly folded her hands and stared Lily down.

Lily dropped her eyes to her lap as she rocked a little faster. "Yes, he did it. I recognized the awful cologne he wears and the shirt he'd had on that day. I knew the man burned his right hand—I saw him squawking as he shook it—and when Nancy came to visit me in the hospital, she told me Peter had hurt his hand and it was all bandaged up so he could hardly write. Peter is right-handed. Yes, it was him. He felt threatened."

"Won't it be hard to face him, knowing that?" asked Hilda.

"No, I can look him straight in the face and smile," Lily said softly. "But he will know, and he will always wonder when I'm coming after him. Always be looking over his shoulder."

"Oh, please don't start up again," Hilda wailed. "You could have told the police, had him locked up for arson."

"A few years for arson after what he's done? No, I'll be very careful this time. And, you know, there have been no more abductions since the fire. But there will be. Men like him can't stop. They can't stop, believe me. Now, lunch must be ready. Come on, let's eat!"

Lily felt light and carefree as she walked to work with her new yellow tote slung over her shoulder. She could face Peter, she could face anything, but she wouldn't have to. Wendy had called just after Magaly and Hilda left. She wanted to know if Lily had ever done any bookkeeping because Peter had just quit, right after Wendy told everyone the good news about Lily coming back. She went out to lunch with Cecil, and by the time she got back, Peter had packed up his things and left. She found a terse note of resignation on her desk. Just like that. Not to worry, Lily had reassured her. It had been a long time, but she had several years of bookkeeping experience. She'd take care of things, perhaps have to learn some different rules, though.

Lily laughed aloud. She already had her nest egg, so Wendy had nothing to worry about—not that she'd cheat Wendy, a good person whom she thought of as part of her new family. They'd all visited and shown they cared. Not Peter, of course, but no one had found that strange. None of them had any idea what she'd been through in her life, no idea of her strength and ability. Especially Peter.

So, back to bookkeeping. Life seemed so circular sometimes. She'd do it right this time. She'd been a silly young
girl back then, thought herself invincible. But she'd been a
great bookkeeper. If only she'd had the wherewithal to go
to college. She would have made a terrific accountant and
could have made her way without leaving all that destruc-
tion in her wake.

*Laura hadn't gone to college straight out of high school.
Her mother had persuaded her father to let her "get out in
the world" before she moved away. Pure spite because her
mother only scraped through twelfth grade—her best friend
told Laura that once.*

*Laura persuaded her father to buy her a couple of dark
suits and crisp blouses to make sure she looked the part and
got a clerical job with a real estate developer. She worked
hard, and they promoted her to assistant bookkeeper after
only three months. She found the work surprisingly satis-
fying, and after only nine months, the bookkeeper went on
maternity leave and she got the job. She turned out to be an
excellent bookkeeper and always maintained a professional
demeanor. The woman had her baby and announced her
intention to return to work after three months. That's when
Laura pointed out to her father how a degree would help
her better herself. She didn't mention she wanted to major
in English, but when that conversation happened, she said
that yes, she wanted to be a teacher. Even her mother liked
that. Respectable to a fault and something to boast about.*

*She'd liked working with numbers, though. You knew
where you were with numbers.*

More Rose. Pansy, actually, as she was known then.
Careful. This was getting too personal.

14

On this beautiful April morning, the daffodil buds showed daubs of yellow. Hilda would be so happy to see her neat garden. Although Lily owned the house, she still thought of it as Hilda's. The old woman had made such a home for herself, and then for Lily. Her no-good son annoyed Lily to no end with his whining. He had no idea how lucky he'd been, no idea. Probably the father's contempt hadn't allowed her children to see their mother in the best light and Hilda would have been too proud to do anything about it. Had Lily's own mother been as bad as her father said? Lily had never really looked at the woman, except with the contempt she learned at her father's knee. Maybe he'd worn her down, stripped her of self-worth and feeling, turned her into the sloven she remembered.

Three weeks of keeping the books and already an old pro. Lily enjoyed the work, its precision and certainty. She didn't want to work full time and fortunately found she could manage the load in four days a week. She turned the corner and stopped short, her breath deserting her for a moment. Two police cars were outside the shop, and a cop stood guard outside. He looked right at her. Too late to go back. She walked slowly to the door.

"What's going on?"

"Who are you, ma'am?"

"Lily Porter, I work here."

"Go inside. They'll want to talk to you."

"About what?"

No answer except an opened door and a jerk of his head. Everyone turned and looked at her, silent and stricken. Wendy spoke first.

"Lily, something terrible has happened. A man kidnapped Nancy's little Ellie last night."

Lily made for her desk, almost staggering. "No, not that monster, not Ellie! What happened?" No one spoke. "Tell me what happened!"

The police had started their interviews in Wendy's office, so Steve filled her in. Nancy and her husband had gone to a neighbor's house. When the doorbell rang, Cindy came into the hallway, but it was Ellie who answered the door. A masked man pushed his way in and grabbed the child. He ran out into the night and must have had a car waiting. There was no trace of her and no ransom demand. "Poor little tyke," Steve said, his voice throaty.

Should she tell what she suspected? Should she go it alone? They hadn't found anything last time, and probably wouldn't now, and Ellie could die. She'd give them the chance, then take matters into her own hands if things didn't work out.

When it came to Lily's turn, she told the cop about Peter, his behavior with Ellie when she'd come into the shop with her mother, and that she'd considered his behavior odd. He'd abruptly quit his job a few weeks ago, too.

"We'll look into it, ma'am."

She certainly hoped so. The shop closed for the day, and Lily returned home, sick and angry as she thought of Ellie's ordeal, Nancy's fear. A child betrayed, a child alone, mauled and tainted by a monster. He'd pay, one way or the other. He'd pay.

Peter would expect Lily to watch him. She called Magaly and told her what happened. "I know it was him, I know it. I'll have to do something to help that child."

"Take care, Lily, do not make Peter do anything rash. Come on over to our place. We will have dinner. We will make a plan."

Hilda sat in the corner, contributing nothing but her qualms as Lily and Magaly talked over their strategy.

"We will do it, Lily, we will do it!" Magaly sounded as if she were looking forward to it. "Now, let us watch the news."

"Police are questioning a man in the case of the kidnapping of Ellie Trent."

"Well, Magaly, let's wait and see. Maybe they won't need us after all."

Laura remembered lying in bed pretending to be asleep. She'd darted back to her bed and kept very still under the covers while he checked to make sure she was asleep. She didn't want him to know she'd been spying on him—the punishment would have been harsh.

The year she turned fifteen, she decided she must say something, and should have long before. Her mother didn't believe her when she started to tell her—in halting words, probably the wrong words because she didn't know the right ones—why she didn't want to spend the summer with her aunt and uncle anymore.

"You wicked girl, saying such terrible things about my brother! Don't you dare talk about this again, to me and certainly not to anyone else!" And that was the end of the story for her mother, but at least she didn't make her go back.

Her aunt died while Laura was in college and her uncle married a widow with two young girls not long after. Should she pay a visit? Look out for them? Talk to them? No one should just avert their eyes from such a thing. Sometime. One of these days.

15

Ellie's heart hadn't stopped thumping from when Peter snatched her. She hadn't known what to think. He'd come to the door with a funny black scarf over his face. Then he whispered his name, and she was so happy to see him she gave him a big hug. Cindy, following behind, screamed when Peter threw a blanket over Ellie's head, put her under his arm, ran out with her, and threw her into the back of his car, shoving her in so hard it hurt. She heard the engine start and tires screech as they sped away.

"Why did you do that, Peter?" she'd cried out.

"Because I know your parents don't want you anymore, but I want you. You're a lovely little girl, and you're going to be my very own little girl for the rest of your life. Stay on the floor and keep that blanket over you. And shut up!"

He'd been smiling back at her while he said it, but when she started to cry, his face turned ugly. She could see it in the mirror. He turned into a side street and stopped.

"Come here. Now."

Ellie stood up behind the front seat. Peter stuck his face very close to hers and said, "Shut up or I'll have to punish you. And you won't like it. Lie down, now, and keep that blanket over your head."

She lay down again and soon felt the car moving. He'd brought her to this place, this great big cold white room.

"We're going to pretend it's your birthday today. You told me you'll turn nine next month. Here, open your presents, and then we'll cut the cake."

"I don't want to, Peter. I want to go home. Take me home."

"You ungrateful little brat! Do you know what happens to little girls like you? They end up in big, big trouble and they get hurt. Be grateful for your presents and don't cry. It makes me really mad, and you won't like me when I'm mad."

Ellie took a half-sobbing deep breath. His face scared her. Not nice and smiley anymore, all teeth and staring eyes. She knew Peter could hurt her. He wasn't the person she'd thought. Her parents had told her she couldn't play outside alone anymore because a bad man was taking children and hurting them. Could that be Peter? She'd have to do whatever he wanted. Perhaps those others hadn't listened. She made herself smile. She must be a good girl.

"I'm sorry, Peter. I like having a special birthday. I'll try to be good."

"That's more like it. We two will be together always if you're good. We can move away from here later to a nicer place. And when you're old enough, we can get married. You'd like to get married, wouldn't you?"

"Yes, Peter," Ellie whispered, although she couldn't picture such a thing, especially with someone like Peter. She and her friends loved to play with Barbie dolls in wedding dresses and pretend to be in a dress just like it, with everyone gazing at them saying how pretty they looked. But they never imagined anything like this. Nothing like this.

"Here, Ellie. Put on this party dress. I bought it especially for you."

It was white and frilly. She didn't know any kids who wore a dress like this.

"Put it on. I'll help you."

She didn't want him touching her or seeing her without her clothes on, but she did as she was told. He helped her take off her jeans and top, stroking her all over as he did. He did it gently, but she knew it was wrong. Her teacher had told the whole class about good touching and bad touching. This was the bad kind. But who could she tell? He slipped the new dress over her head and did up all the buttons at the back slowly, stopping sometimes to stroke her hair.

"There, you see. Beautiful. My lovely little bride. Pretty girls should never wear jeans, you know. I'll get you lots of gorgeous dresses. I didn't hear you say thank you!"

His voice changed to angry when he said that about the thank you, so she said it quickly and with her widest pretty smile. He turned nice again.

Peter pushed a slice of cake at her, which she nibbled at, pretending to enjoy it. She opened her presents—a doll and some books—and thanked him. He gave her another one, a big shaggy toy dog.

"That's your special friend for when I have to go out."

"Thank you, Peter."

The dog was soft and cuddly and holding it made her feel better. Peter's smell all mixed in with the cake was beginning to make her feel bad. She told herself she was a strong girl and if she could just be nice, not make him mad, maybe she could get away later. She held the dog tighter. She decided his name was Max, like the one at home, only the Max at home was real.

Peter told her he was going to take a nap on the bed in the corner, and would she like to join him? She shook her head, but when his face turned crazy again, she nodded instead.

"That's better. We'll just pretend we're married. You don't have to take your dress off this time. Just cuddle up with me."

Ellie trailed behind him and lay down on the bed next to him. He gazed into her eyes.

"Close your eyes now, Ellie. Go to sleep."

She closed her eyes. She could feel him fidgeting around, making funny sounds. He sounded as if he had a pain, but she didn't open her eyes to find out. His smell was so strong here, and she had to concentrate on not throwing up—that would really make him mad. She must have fallen asleep for a while because she jumped when he shook her.

"Wake up, Ellie, I'm going out. I might be gone for some time, but you have cake to eat and plenty of toys to play with. You're such a pretty little girl, and you've been good, too, not like the others. I'll be back."

He went to a sink in the corner she hadn't noticed until now. He washed his hands, then opened his pants and washed down there, too. She quickly turned her head away. How disgusting. And embarrassing. He noticed and smiled.

"You'll soon get used to everything about me, Ellie," he said. "And you'll learn to like it. You'd better."

"Yes, Peter."

"And this is your potty," he said with a nasty smile, pointing to a white, covered thing in a corner she'd thought was a chair.

He left and slammed the door behind him. She heard a sort of snap, then his footsteps going away and the sound of the car. It was safe to let the tears out now, and she cried for a very long time. When she was all out of tears, she wiped her eyes on her sleeve and looked around. She should see what she could find. She searched in vain for a key, tried the door just in case, screamed for her mother, but nothing.

Ellie hugged her new toy dog, her face pressing into its fuzzy back, but she lifted her head after a while and wrinkled her nose. The fur had a funny smell, something sharp and, after a while, nasty. She supposed he was made of fake fur, like one of Cindy's jackets, and that didn't smell so good, either.

She tasted the salty tears that ran again as she thought of her warm, pink bedroom. She looked around. The room had walls made of rough gray blocks and a slippery floor, although Peter had covered the part she crouched on with the sort of mat they had in the bathroom at her house. It was better than sitting on the icy bare floor. She looked at the bed. She didn't want to go back there. He'd done yucky things there, and she was sure that if she could still smell him a bit over here, it would be much worse over there. Peter put scent on his face, sort of like ladies put behind their ears, only not nice, not nice at all, like flowers that had been in the trash for a long time. She could see now that nothing about Peter was nice. She had to think about other things. Not Peter. She mustn't be crying when he got back, or he'd hurt her.

Ellie looked around and up, but saw only a white ceiling with a spider's web in one corner; she couldn't see its owner. She wasn't afraid of spiders. She'd read Charlotte's Web over and over. She had goose bumps now. It was getting colder. It must be nighttime. She frightened herself thinking about the dark outside. It was too bright in here, but better than too dark. She'd never been in a place before where she couldn't hear anything. No voices, no traffic, no television, no nothing. Was being dead like this? Cold. Silent. Lonesome.

She got up to move around. She thought of putting the itchy hairy blanket from the bed around her shoulders, but oh, that stink. She clutched the toy dog for warmth and wandered around the room, touching everything as she went. Her fingers scraped over the rough wall and slid across a hard metal box. She tried the lid. Locked. She sat the new doll on the box and stroked her silky hair. Its painted face seemed to watch her wherever she moved in the room. The doll's face wasn't friendly at all, but she shouldn't be surprised because Peter had chosen her. She picked up an old book and tossed it down. She might look at it later, although it was a bit babyish for her.

There was more birthday cake on the wobbly little brown table, but Ellie didn't feel hungry. She hadn't been hungry earlier, either, but she knew how angry Peter would have been if she hadn't shown she appreciated her birthday party. Looking at the cake's squishy sweet frosting, she felt she might be sick, could already taste it in the back of her throat, but clenched her teeth and forced it down. The potty stood alone in the corner, and she could feel it waiting for her, just like that spider hid up there, waiting patiently for what it knew must happen. She didn't want to use it, because it wouldn't be private like at home, and she couldn't flush. Peter would see what she'd done and smell it, too. But she had to go.

After Ellie finished, she cuddled the furry dog and curled up on the mat. She closed her eyes and sucked her thumb hard and fast, something she hadn't done for years and years, ever since she'd become a big girl. Her thumb tasted good and smelled good, too. It helped block out this terrible place, this hard, stinky place. She'd stopped crying hours ago. Used up all her tears. Too tired and cold now to cry.

Ellie lost track of days and nights. The light was always the same in here. Peter came and went. He brought hamburgers and fries, and sometimes something different. He brought her more dresses, but she had to take them off for the naps, now. He stroked her and then did his fidgeting and funny noises while she pretended to be asleep. He didn't hurt her, though, and she never peeked. She knew she wouldn't like what he was doing, although she couldn't imagine what it might be. She'd gotten used to his smell, hardly even noticed it anymore.

Then he came in one day looking frightened and crazy. He looked at her for a long time. He put his hands around her neck and his eyes sort of popped out as he stared into hers. She sensed deep down he might really hurt her, without knowing exactly how. Ellie, too numb to move, forced herself to get her mind working, make it work smart. She looked into his eyes and smiled at him, pulled up her best smile. His eyes closed for a moment and he rushed out, locking her in again. Ellie tried the door again—knowing it was no use; she'd heard the lock turn—and turned back to the little rug as she started to shake, finding more tears than she thought she had left.

Peter didn't come back. She didn't know how long it had been, only that she was very hungry. She found some fries in the trash. They didn't taste good, but better than nothing. The water in the tap tasted funny, like metal. She found a packet of cookies on a shelf. She'd eat just one and only when she absolutely had to. Later, after she'd nibbled away the last one, she curled up on the bed under the blanket and sucked her thumb. Even Peter's smell didn't seem so bad now. At least it was the smell of a person, better than nothingness.

He was never coming for her. She knew that now. She may as well go to sleep.

16

"A person of interest has been arrested in the case of the kidnapping of Ellie Trent." A picture of Steve flashed on the screen.

"No," Lily yelled, slamming her hand on her lap. "No!"

She called Magaly. "I know he didn't do it. Something funny's going on. And they haven't mentioned Peter. They've never mentioned him by name, either. Magaly, we'll have to hold off a bit longer. We need to get a better idea of the situation."

"You are right, Lily, but I am still going to hold on to your costume."

"He lives closer to me, Magaly. I'll pay for a taxi for you if—when—it comes time."

"No need, no need."

Lily called Wendy.

"What's going on with Steve, Wendy?"

"He just called. They've released him, Lily. He had an alibi—for Ellie's kidnapping and another."

"Another?"

"He was found in that park off Davenport, beaten up. He didn't see who did it. They took him to the hospital and found a child's locket around his neck. It belonged to the last victim before Ellie. He swore he didn't know where it came from, but they didn't believe him. They still suspect he's involved, though."

"My God, I can't believe Steve would do anything like that!"

"No, me neither. But he does have a watertight alibi. He was at church, singing in the choir!"

"Steve? Church choir? You're kidding!"

"I know. Turns out he's been going to that church all his life."

"Of course, singing in a church choir would ruin his reputation. No wonder he kept it quiet."

They laughed, then stopped abruptly, realizing how their mirth seemed outlandish in the midst of Ellie's horror.

"The kid was set up, Wendy."

"Well, it's a bit of a coincidence that there's a connection to my shop, don't you think?"

No, not at all. Peter was trying to be clever. She would have to be more so.

"I don't believe in coincidences. But Steve didn't do it, I'm sure of that."

"You know I can't fire him, but I'm not comfortable having him in the shop. People won't come in if they recognize him."

"Well, have him do inventory in the back. I can come out and help with customers if need be. I'm sure he'll understand."

Yes, that's how it would be. Always that cloud, that seed of doubt. Steve didn't deserve that. She'd fix things. She would. She ought to call Nancy and see if she knew.

The conversation stumbled. Nancy had been notified, but she didn't seem surprised or hopeful. She sounded flat, numb.

"Nancy, is your husband with you? Is Cindy?"

"He is and he isn't. He's in his chair, dead drunk. Cindy? She's going out at six, she's out all the time, doesn't listen to me, it's as if she doesn't care about her sister. I think she's seeing someone, but she won't tell me anything. I feel so alone, Lily, so alone."

"Nancy, you need some support just now. Come over here anytime you want, stay over. I've plenty of room."

"Thanks, Lily. I keep hoping she'll walk through the door. I guess that isn't going to happen though, is it? Wish I knew what Cindy was up to. I can't lose her as well."

"Well, remember, Nancy, anytime."

Lily sat thinking. He wouldn't go for someone Cindy's age, would he? She got up and put her coat on. She could get round to Nancy's before six. She got out her black hooded jacket, a scarf, and rubber-soled shoes.

She walked as fast as she could and selected a corner where she had Nancy's house in full view. Ten minutes to spare. These spring evenings were chilly. In Northern Virginia, it would probably be balmy right now. *No, Lily, no comparisons, no sense to it.* Nancy's front door slammed and Lily pulled her hood over her forehead and her scarf across her mouth. Dressed in a short dress with a low-cut top entirely unsuited to the climate, Cindy tottered along on high heels as if she'd had her feet bound—absurd and sweet. She was moving in the opposite direction, so Lily followed at a safe distance. A car waited on the next street, engine idling, and the driver got out and opened the passenger door for Cindy. Lily sidled closer. The man kissed her on the lips, and she looked up at him adoringly. Cecil. "I've got champagne on ice at my place," she heard him say.

A phone call was all it would take. Underage girl in his apartment. She had the shop key on the ring with her house keys. She'd find his address, call the cops, and tell them where to find Cecil and his little conquest. Slimy bastard! Hell and damnation, who would help her with her novel now?

The doorbell rang. She wasn't expecting anyone, better be careful. Lily looked through the peephole. Nancy.

"Any news?"

"No, not Ellie. Just Cindy. Do you know she's been having an affair with Cecil? Of all people, that effete little creep!"

"Oh no, Nancy, that's disgusting. What happened?"

"The police got an anonymous tip that he was seducing underage girls and they caught him red-handed. With our daughter!" Nancy's voice hovered near hysteria.

"I'm so sorry. What did you do?"

"There's nothing I can do, is there? She blamed me for tattling, but I didn't know. How could I? How could she do this with her little sister in grave danger? How could she, damn it?"

"It's just as well he's been stopped. I bet it's not the first time. You have to wonder why he really left his last job. And your husband, what did he do?"

"He had another drink. What else would he do? I made dinner tonight, and they both sat there sulking. Cindy wouldn't answer me when I asked her if she'd like some potatoes, and Tom got mad when I told her to show some respect. Said I should stop picking on her. I picked up the dish of potatoes and threw it at the wall over Cindy's head. Then I picked up the pan of stew and emptied it into Tom's lap. And then I came here."

"Stay as long as you like, Nancy. You need some rest, some peace. Have you been able to sleep?"

"No, I'm at the end of my tether. How can I sleep when my baby might be cold and frightened? Or..." Nancy broke down then, her grief gaining momentum until she was almost screaming.

"Shh, Nancy, shh, let's stay positive. It's only been a week. And she's a smart girl. I'm going to give you something to help you sleep. You'll be no good to anyone if you fall apart."

Time for action. Only a week, but long enough.

Nancy's grief shook Lily. That's how parents should feel, of course, but she'd never actually seen such a visceral display. She thought of how she felt when she'd seen that news report and thought Andrew might be dead, that leaden hole in her mind. Had she caused people to feel that kind of deep despair? Definitely.

She'd turned a nook off the kitchen into her writing space. It overlooked the garden and proved an ideal spot for the peace she needed to concentrate. She'd snuggle there after Nancy fell asleep and write about this for her novel. The heroine would suffer this kind of grief because she thought her love was dead. Finally, she could put some real feelings in her work. Although grief for a lover wouldn't be the same thing, would it? Maybe her heroine should have a little sister. But look at Cindy. What a heartless little bitch she turned out to be. Maybe that was her way of staving off fear. People were way too complicated. That's the thing about romance novels: complications get resolved, everyone feels what they should feel, and everyone lives happily ever after. No wonder people liked them so much.

She would find Andrew one of these days. She couldn't reveal herself, but he probably wouldn't recognize her now, anyway. She needed her son.

Laura always looked forward to Thanksgiving. Her father sounded so sad when she told him over the phone she wouldn't be able to make it. He said he understood, and she knew he did. Her mother would not be able to resist indulging in a litany of recrimination and it would spoil the day for everyone.

Thanksgiving at her cousin Andy's house would be fun. He was to shop and she would cook, although he was sure to forget something, necessitating last-minute forays to the convenience store for what she lacked. They could always laugh about things, though.

She worried about Andy sometimes. He'd been devastated after his mother died. A staid, solemn young man, he needed harmony and a mother's touch. She wished he'd find the right woman. She wished him great happiness. But he still seemed so sad. He'd be hard-pressed to find happiness, and he might not be able to grasp it should it come his way. Poor, dear Andy, staid on the outside, but sensitive to a fault once you got past his layers of postures.

Here we go again. She'd written very similar words in the journal.

17

F our o'clock, right on time. Lily watched Peter lock his front door before shoving his fists into his jacket pockets and heading down toward St. Claire, shoulders hunched against the wind. She'd been watching him for three days, and each day he'd left home at this time, first picking up coffee at Tim Horton's, then buying pizza at Charlie's. No wonder he was so pudgy and pasty. She could follow him. He might be going to Ellie. But he might have abandoned her, too, so they must act swiftly. In any case, Magaly would be following him at a distance, so with any luck, this was just his normal routine. She picked the lock and entered, careful to lock the door behind her.

The house smelled of dirty socks, although dust-free and surprisingly neat. She wanted to search the place, especially the drawers and closets, but she should put on her costume and make sure to be ready by the time he got back. She climbed the stairs and looked around. Three bedrooms and one bathroom. The smallest bedroom held some boxes and an iron cot. She'd hide in there.

Lily opened her hold-all and got out the clown costume Magaly rented for her. She'd opted out of clown shoes—too clumsy—and wore black oxfords. And no greasepaint, as she would need to make a quick getaway. She'd tried on the mask at home and could put that on at the last minute, the white gloves, too. Fingerprints without ridges could also be a giveaway. She went into the biggest bedroom and looked in the mirror. She looked the part. She remembered reading an article in the Star about people who dress up as clowns and entertain sick children. You could be anyone in this getup. Say anything, do silly things, feel carefree, make a child laugh. Not tonight, though; she'd be her old self tonight.

Did Peter sleep in this room? It looked as if he slept in the middle bedroom with its geode collection and half-open closet, pajamas folded on the pillow, a pair of leather slippers next to the bed. This room was all pink and frilly. Very neat, bed made, furniture polished, fresh flowers. A place to keep little girls? The mother's bedroom; of course, the mother. Something strange here. At least the bed was a four-poster. Perfect. Lily shuddered and went back to her hidey-hole.

She fingered the lengths of rope, holding them like rose stems. How on earth would Magaly get him upstairs? She didn't feel like pulling his dead weight, but they needed a bed. The tricky part would be disabling him. He might be soft, but he was big. If only she'd been able to get hold of chloroform. Hitting him, she'd deemed risky—too easy to overdo or underestimate. He needed to be out of commission for a while, but not too long. Well, Magaly's pepper spray would have to do. The old girl had bought it on the street the year before, and even sprayed a little against Lily's kitchen wall to make sure it worked; they stood too close and their eyes burned for a good half-hour. Lily pulled out the recorder and checked the tape. One-two-three echoed back. Good. She set out the alcohol and matches. Ah yes, water, just in case. She'd noticed the bathroom next door. She looked around the pink-tiled, -carpeted, and -papered bathroom. No shower curtain—and no shower, how odd, especially for a man—but a pitcher sat on the corner of the tub. Perhaps he used it for rinsing his hair. She filled the pitcher with water and took it back to her hidey-hole.

Maybe they should have confided in Steve and got him involved. They'd decided against it. He was in enough trouble, and impetuous besides. Lily took some deep breaths.

The door and voices. She'd done it, she got in. Good old Magaly. Lily donned her mask, her breath coming faster as she waited to play her role.

"Peter, your dear mother spoke so adoringly of you. You were the apple of her eye!"

"I don't remember Mother ever mentioning you, Mrs. Sauger. And you knew her before she got married, you say? So, how did you know about me?"

"Oh, dear boy, we wrote to each other every month. We used a post office box because she said we had to keep our friendship a secret. Please, Peter, do not take this the wrong way, but it was almost as if she was afraid of him."

"She was. He treated her very badly. Me, too." *How on earth did Magaly know that?*

"Oh, I am sorry to hear that. And then, suddenly, nothing. I wrote four or five letters, then got them back, stamped 'no longer at this address.' Of course, now I know she died."

"When was that, Mrs. Sauger?" Lily held her breath.

"Oh, I do not quite remember, many years ago." Well done!

"She left town for a bit. When she came back, she was ill."

"Oh, I am so sorry, dear Peter. Do you have any photographs of my dear Elizabeth?" Thank heavens they'd searched the birth registry for Peter. Lily already knew his parents were dead and Peter lived in the house he grew up in. Taciturn as he was, he'd mumbled a few replies to her early attempts to be friendly.

"I'll go upstairs and get some for you. Then you can tell me about my mother when she was a girl. Was she happy in those days? I know she was pretty." His voice sounded eager, wistful, breathy.

"I will come up with you. I would like to see her room."

"Oh, I don't think…"

"Please, dear Peter, please. I loved your mother so much. I would like to feel close to her."

Peter grunted and Lily heard heavy footsteps plod up the stairs and the door to the large bedroom open. At Peter's screech, Lily dashed in, ropes ready. Peter cowered in a corner, clutching his eyes as Magaly, a hilarious sight in horn-rimmed spectacles and bright red lipstick, threatened him with her cane. They followed their plan on how to move him, one clutching him under each arm as they dragged him to the bed. He put up a good fight until Magaly sprayed him again and the pain rendered him almost helpless. Tying him up still wasn't easy, until, "You want more spray, Peter?" from Magaly convinced him to stop struggling. He fought again as Lily took his second hand away from his eyes, which streamed and blinked and strained. Once he seemed securely tied, Lily went and fetched her meager equipment.

"Go now," she told Magaly. "Are you okay?" Magaly couldn't seem to catch her breath, coughing and sputtering like an old car engine.

Magaly took a deep breath and winced. "I will be fine. I have got allergies. Sure you will be all right alone with this one?" Lily nodded. "Goodbye, dear Peter!" Magaly threw him a toothy smile.

"What do you want?" Peter screamed. "What do you want, you crazy old woman?"

Lily listened to the footsteps descend, slow and heavy. When she heard the front door slam, she pulled up a little vanity chair and sat by the bed. She opened the bottle of rubbing alcohol and poured it over Peter's crotch. He jumped as the cold wet registered. "What the fuck?"

"Funny you should say that, Peter." Lily set her voice deeper, harsher.

He seemed to register for the first time that a different kind of someone was in the room. He squinted at her, his face a comic mask of horror as his sight cleared enough to take in the clown. He coughed and trembled.

"You see, Peter, I want to know what you've been doing with those little girls. And I want to know where you've got Ellie."

"What do you know about Ellie?"

"I know you took her. I want her back. I'm going to turn on this recorder and you are going to talk. Or else."

"Fuck you!"

"Or else I set fire to the alcohol I just poured on your crotch."

Peter, his eyes a little wider now, looked down at the wetness on his pants and moaned. Lily struck a match.

"No, no! I'll tell you where to find Ellie. And I never touched those girls until after, when it didn't matter anymore. They wouldn't keep quiet, they wouldn't be nice. I had to do something. Wasn't my fault."

"Go on." Lily blew out the match and switched on the recorder. "Talk!"

And talk he did, rambling on about his need to groom a wife, how he loved his mother, how lonely he felt.

"Peter, what about Ellie?"

"Probably too late, haven't seen her in a few days. Expect she's hungry."

"Where is she, damn it?" Lily struck another match, holding it carefully to make it last.

He described the warehouse, gave Lily an address on the other side of town. She turned off the recorder. She looked at him. She'd like to stay longer, punish him some more, but she had to get word to the police fast. Lily dropped the match, almost spent, in Peter's lap and watched the flames spread as Peter's screams rose to hysteria. It was only rubbing alcohol, so would play itself out soon. She hurried back to the little room to change before getting out of the house.

She'd call the police from a call box. His keening got on her nerves now, so before she left she went back in and dumped the cold water over his scorched pants. "Better?" she asked, but Peter only gasped and wept for his mother.

Good, the call box on the corner stood empty. "What is your emergency?" She adopted her father's plummy English accent, told them where a kidnapped child could be found, gave them Ellie's name, and Peter's, and hung up. Next, she tucked the tape inside the padded envelope she'd prepared and dropped it into the first mailbox she came to. She had to walk the fifteen blocks home, but the early evening air felt good and rid her nostrils of the nasty frying smell. All things considered, willy flambé seemed a fitting end to Peter's life as a pedophile.

She heard it on the late news. Acting on an anonymous tip, the police found Ellie in a storage unit, barely alive. She'd been taken to the hospital and was expected to make a full recovery. Peter Bachman of Toronto was under arrest. Lily called a cab and woke up Nancy, who'd spent most of her time sleeping the past few days. Nancy, shaky and teary, blew her a kiss as she left the house.

Lily smiled and leaned back in her recliner, drained. She ought to eat, but didn't have much of an appetite. Such a horrid smell. How had her nosy old landlady smelled, burning up in that old house? Papery, moldy. That teacher, too, the one she'd forgotten might be at home. On the rare occasions Lily looked back on her early life, she always felt as if she were looking down the wrong end of a telescope, a portal to a surreal and distant world she'd left far behind. Not so far behind, perhaps.

She called Magaly early the next morning. "You see the news?"

"Yes, it worked out good." Magaly coughed.

"You were magnificent, Magaly."

"As were you, my dear. Come over for dinner tonight. I will make goulash." She coughed again and sounded short of breath. Lily hoped she meant stuffed peppers. Her friend was getting old, or perhaps she felt more stressed by the whole Peter affair than she let on. And that cough worried her.

The shop sported pink balloons, a huge basket of chrysanthemums, and a mélange of chatter and laughter. Wendy said she'd spring for dinner for everyone later. Ellie was safe. Nancy had taken a cab to the hospital as soon as she heard and stayed by her child's bedside. Even Wendy—depressed since Cecil's arrest—had cheered up. "Peter, Cecil—I've been harboring monsters!" she said. *You have no idea*, Lily couldn't help thinking with a smile.

Wendy had phoned one of the detectives who questioned them after Ellie's disappearance, and he gave her a few details on the quiet. He asked her out on a date, too! He said he would tell her more over dinner. Apparently, they'd found Ellie still clutching a toy dog and surrounded by toys. Only wearing a thin party dress, the poor child was suffering from hypothermia. There was plenty of evidence against Peter, who lay in a prison hospital being treated for burns and could say nothing other than some gibberish about an evil clown.

Later that night, Lily thought about her novel. She hadn't been in the mood after her clown act and had stuck it in her desk drawer. Maybe she could manage a few paragraphs.

Laura remembered the rage she let loose after a few counseling sessions, the last one of which included her mother. It never occurred to the woman to blame herself for letting it happen. It never occurred to her to feel ashamed for not listening, for letting her brother do that to his niece, to feel sorry for her daughter's pain. Her family's reputation was all that concerned her. Maybe it happened to her years ago—he was a lot older than his sister, after all. Maybe she was scared of him, or maybe her mother hadn't listened, either. Her mother's betrayal angered Laura more than his. He was just a rotten pervert, but she was a mother, for God's sake! A mother who, even then, didn't confront her brother and who made Laura quit counseling. But at least she didn't have to go to that house anymore, that ordinary house that always smelled of lemon-scented polish. To this day, that smell made her want to retch. Her mother smacked Laura around the face when she threw out the cans from their supply cupboard.

"They use it at that house. It makes me sick. You make me sick." They'd never talked much after that. Perhaps her mother couldn't face her own truth.

Close to the bone. Too close. Laura deserved her own life, not a sad sack version of Lily's.

18

Lily's face pulled and stung with every twitch. Laughing and smiling, once grudging nods to Rose's social requirements had come to feel normal. Since her facial surgeries, they'd become uncomfortable again—physically, though. If her bandages didn't come off soon, she might take a step back into her other self, one whose pleasant face had been a mask. She'd almost forgotten how to enjoy eating, too. This should be the last surgery, thank heavens, and she hoped she would look good. She wasn't so old that she didn't want to look good. She didn't want a man, but it seemed important to know she could get one if she wanted to. Complicated and unnecessary, but it was so. She looked different, and that was the most important thing. No more looking over her shoulder. No way of identifying her unless they got her DNA. It would be on file, but she didn't plan to give anyone an excuse to use it.

Oh, God, she wanted to sneeze and she couldn't even hold her nose. Shelving books kicked up dust, but Nancy had taken a few months off to stay with Ellie and the new clerk had been caught pilfering the petty cash, so they were shorthanded. Lily left a pile of books on the floor and went back to her desk. Wendy was interviewing a candidate in her office and Lily hoped she would pass muster. A small job, but one that could change a life.

"Steve, I can't shelve anymore. The dust is making my nose itch. I can't let myself sneeze, it hurts too much."

"Okay, Lily, I'm nearly done." Steve crammed the last of his sandwich in his mouth, his cheeks bulging as he mangled their load, none too quietly. The shop door jangled. "Mmm…" as he pointed at his burden. "Out in a sec," he mumbled behind a napkin.

Lily rounded the corner into the main shop floor in time to hear, "Anyone home?" A booming, hearty man's voice, one that squeezed Lily's chest. Toby. *Pull yourself together. Most of your face is bandaged.*

"Good morning, sir. So sorry, we're a little shorthanded. Can I help you?"

"Yes, I want to read some Canadian authors. I've just moved into the neighborhood. I'm from the US of A, you know."

As if you couldn't tell, given his southern propensity for putting his vowels to the rack.

"What kinds of books do you like to read? We have some good mysteries over here. Or biographies, perhaps?"

"I like a good mystery. Nothing too gory, mind. I'm not into that these days…" Lily could imagine the rest of that thought. Her throat parched, she struggled to open her voice.

"Here's an author I enjoy. She sets her books in small towns in Ontario. The violence tends to be offstage, although there's more action than in most cozies. I think you'll find them fast-paced and entertaining." Lily hoped the parts of her face that showed weren't sweaty enough to notice.

"Thank you." He read the front cover flap of one and picked up several more. "I'll take these. If you don't mind my asking..." He gestured with incongruous delicacy toward her face. "Accident?"

"Yes, a fire in my apartment. One of those old wood houses. But these will come off soon." A simple yes would have sufficed.

"I'm sorry. I look forward to seeing what you really look like! You have a lovely voice." He looked disappointed when Lily only responded with Rose's cool half-smile and a nod. "I'll come and see you again when I need some new additions to my library. My new place is a lovely old stone house. It has two big apartments I'm renovating. I've got a place in Florida. Weather's great, but I'm really bored with it and I'll be coming up here on business more and more. I'm making a study for myself with lots of bookshelves. It's even got a fireplace!"

The old Toby, childlike in his enthusiasm, grinned and ambled out, leaving Lily clutching the till for support as her mind reeled through those scenes—Samantha's bloodied head on the floor of her garage, Toby sagging with grief after her funeral—which Rose had thankfully missed while she cavorted in the Caribbean with Janet. Then the humiliations at that hospital for the criminally insane in Nowhere, Virginia.

"You all right?" Steve's ready concern brought her back.

"Oh, yes. Thanks. I think I need to eat something. Skipped breakfast. Silly of me."

The walk back to her desk was a hard slog, much like wading through quicksand. The chair squeaked in protest as she dropped. She wanted to rest her face in her hands, but she couldn't take the pain. She closed her eyes. Plot the next scene in her novel. That always took her mind to another place, a safer place. Damn Cecil, the creep had been a good teacher, helped her quite a bit. Perhaps she could find another class somewhere. She heard Wendy's office door open. *Pull yourself together. They said you are a cold-blooded killer. So act the part!* She got her sandwich from the fridge and unwrapped it as if tearing the foil might set off a bomb. She tore off a small piece of the soft bread and inched it into her mouth. Eating hurt, they all knew that, so they wouldn't realize her stomach's new reluctance to accept its new reality. Why was she so shaken? Even with the bandages off, no one would recognize her. Paranoia, pure and simple. Was there no end to this fear, this compelling need for eternal vigilance?

He said he liked her voice. Her voice. Toby might come to recognize it as familiar. Its American tones and occasional British inflections might trigger a bitter memory. She'd lost most of her hair. Once dark, it had grown back salt and pepper. Perhaps some highlights? She'd always worn it off her face. A style that covered her cheeks would be good. But that would take time.

She could avoid Toby for the most part. But he lived in the neighborhood. He was a problem. Her breath quickened, heat rose behind her eyes and blurred her vision, her stomach knotted, her fists clenched. No, all that was over, finished. *Take a deep breath, get control, force it down.* She must not do anything that might attract attention. Nothing that would make the cops look into Toby's background. The Ellie problem had been bad enough. Ellie. *You did something good there. You saved a little girl. Too bad I couldn't save my own sister. Well, I did, but not the right way.* She could have gotten help, but was only a kid herself. Killing her wasn't the only way. Killing any of them, lashing out like a cornered rat, was never the answer. *I stole my own life along with theirs.*

Lily finished the day, moving through her tasks as if an unwelcome guest in her own body. Night was the planning time. Her bed, command central.

Where was Andrew? She needed him. She'd find him soon.

Lily sat at her desk again, determined to get on with her novel. Her voice. Her voice might give her away. She'd think it all through later, in bed. In the meantime, she needed to give her hero his voice as Laura first heard it, after the headmaster announced the appointment. She'd really have to work on getting some kind of order into this. His speech belonged right near the beginning.

> "Good afternoon, everyone. I know this is slightly awkward for you all, to be confronted with a new headmaster in such an abrupt fashion. I would ask that we all make every effort to make the transition as smooth as possible. I have already met with Tina Golan and had extensive conversations with her regarding not only the running of the school, but the traditions and values you all hold dear..." and so it went on as he voiced the requisite sentiments. "I look forward to working with you. I know we'll make a good team. Thank you."

His voice was so mellifluous and sonorous that Laura was sorry he had stopped talking—the air felt emptier, somehow. He had taken her breath away, and she hoped she wouldn't be tongue-tied when it was her turn to meet him. She got up after he left the stage and joined the group of women in the lobby. The men had mostly wandered off, rather disgruntled and uneasy. The women were off balance. Laura saw that they were giggling and chattering too much like the eighth graders who'd been invited to the high school dance. Even old Stephanie Bennett was fluttering. Well, she wasn't much better. That face and that voice! She took a deep breath and composed herself. After spending a few minutes participating in the inanity, she decided to go home.

Good, some progress made. She'd better practice cutting and pasting because she'd written everything out of order. And she must take a good look at those passages too close to her own story. Although, if this was to be some sort of version of the Pansy/Rose/Lily story, then it was an ideal one with a fairy tale ending. Early days yet.

To bed now and to think out a plan. No mistakes this time.

19

“Lily and Steve, I'd like you to meet Natasha. She's going to take on the new sales clerk position, and she'll be helping to improve our computer system, too. She says she can design a website for us on the internet.”

“Cool! Can you teach us how to use it?” Steve, pink and gabby, extended his hand, which Natasha accepted with a toothy smile and a dismissive head-to-toe scan with her slanted eyes.

“Hello, Natasha. I hope you will be very happy here. Sorry if I seem solemn, I can't smile much yet.”

“Well, hello, Steve and Lily. Wendy explained about the burns, Lily. I've got one of my own.” Natasha pulled aside her curtain of black hair to expose a fierce pink pucker all the way down the right edge of her face. “Cosmetic surgery is a luxury where I come from. Not something anyone would want to kiss, is it?”

Stricken by the brutality of both the scar and quip, Steve and Wendy shifted their gaze to the floor. Lily did not. Natasha's taut voice rang as high as a child's, and her accent sounded faintly French. What was her story? She was too young to be a Vietnamese refugee.

"Where was that, Natasha?" The others shifted, taken aback by Lily's bluntness.

"Oh, that story would take me all day. I'll get to it sometime."

"I see." Something dreadful had hardened and sharpened the girl, something she was not ready to share. "Can you teach us to search the internet, use it for research?"

"Of course. You can find just about anything or anyone you want these days."

"I'm looking forward to it." And so she was. Lily returned to her desk and opened the ledgers. She had to find Andrew. Memories of her boy ate into her like a canker these days. She needed to know he was doing well, although happy was perhaps too much to hope for. If she came face-to-face with him, could she pass herself off as someone else? Why did she need him so much and not the others? If it hadn't been for her hellish childhood, she would probably have turned out more like Lucy. But he'd always loved her most, had always shown it with his thoughtful little gifts, always shown his need for her approval. She remembered how he stayed with her for a month after her concussion. Of course, he had no idea at the time of the real story of that accident, that it was she who had bludgeoned Judy to death. Lily smothered a laugh.

"What's so funny?" Steve stood in front of her, half a smile and half a frown lending him the look of a brave child waiting for a shot.

"Just an old memory. Nothing more." She watched him slouch back to his shelving chores, the small hunch of his shoulders telling her he'd just suffered a putdown from Natasha.

A couple of days later, Natasha shut down her laptop and rested her palms on it, peering at Lily from behind her sheet of hair.

"That name, that Andrew, he must be important. Who is he?" Her voice was gentle, cajoling, sly.

Damn, she should have used a fake name until she could get her own computer hooked up to the web. Not that they'd found anything. "No one close, not anymore. The son of an old friend of mine. She died last year and I never even knew she was ill because my own husband was dying. I was always fond of the boy." *Good one!*

"I see." The girl's eyes, the hypervigilant eyes of a street urchin, looked unconvinced.

"Well, thank you so much, Natasha. When I get my own computer hooked up to the internet, I'll try a few more old friends. It's terrible how you let people drift away."

"My people didn't drift away. They were blown away."

Natasha thrust her chin forward like a rebellious teen, turned on her heel, and stalked off. What on earth was with that girl? Offended because she felt Lily hadn't trusted her with the truth? Lily hoped it was only trauma and its contempt for anyone who hadn't suffered. But Lily understood trauma. Did Natasha sense it, like some claimed animals smelled fear?

Lily read in the local paper the week before that the library offered internet service now, for a fee. She'd go right after work.

The doorbell jingled, Lily stuck her head around the office door, and there he was again. Nearly closing time. Her bandages were off except for a wide one across her nose. She waited to see if anyone else would go out.

"Hello, hello, anyone there?"

She drew herself up and walked toward him, watching herself from some safe perch a long way off.

"Oh, hello, Lily. My, you look good today. Just one bandage to go, huh?"

"Yes, I'm coming along."

Toby's demeanor exuded charm. Southern charm for charming a lady. Lily's skin didn't show her age, at least not anymore, but she certainly didn't want a flirtation, not with him, not with anyone.

"Well, in strong light you can see the tight shine from the grafts. I'm going to be 55 next week, after all, so I suppose I should be grateful the wrinkles are pulled out!"

"Really, lovely lady. You don't look a day over forty." But his voice sounded cooler and his charm oozed a little less. "Do you have anything new for me?"

"Actually, I just shelved a couple." Lily led the way. "This one is about a young violinist who has an affair with the conductor, and the ripples it sent throughout the whole symphony."

He turned on her, arms rigid against his body. "God, no. I'm not into symphonies. No happy memories there." Lily recoiled a little, her anxiety registering before she could stop it.

"Sorry, it's just that my wife and I were involved with our local symphony once and something terrible happened. Nothing I want to talk about. Sorry if I startled you."

"That's quite all right, I understand." Given the way he behaved, her own reaction should seem normal. "What about this one? This is set in Alberta. A good deal of corporate espionage and derring-do."

"You know, I always liked your voice. And now, for some reason, it reminds me of someone. I can't remember who."

So here it was. "I'm sure my voice is quite usual. Especially in this country, with our mix of accents, North American and British, especially." That should do it.

"Yes, I suppose you're right. I'll think of it, eventually."

"If you'd care to leave your address, I could drop you a postcard when a book I think you'd like comes in."

"Oh, that would be so kind. Thank you!" Like taking candy from a baby, and without the tears.

Toby scribbled out his address, paid for his book, and left. Lily turned around the 'closed' sign and started to put the store to bed for the night.

Lily appreciated the librarian's kindness and, above all, her patience. She used the name of a minor celebrity this time. As soon as the woman felt she was able to manage alone, she began her search for Andrew. He would have changed his name slightly, she was sure. And here he was. Clever boy, not very different, but different enough. A. Simon Hale, Blayton, & Boggs, P.C., Seattle, Washington, complete with address and general phone number. She felt she should have been able to find his home address and phone number, but couldn't get to it. Well, all in good time. She'd find a reason to call, just to hear his voice. She must get her own internet connection hooked up soon. She'd spend the afternoon writing. A hero's tale, this time. A white knight. And something completely new. No makeovers.

Laura inhaled the crisp air, enjoying the sting of smoke from a wood fire in her nostrils. She'd get a house with a fireplace one day. She remembered reading Agatha Christie mysteries with worthy villagers being served tea and crumpets—perhaps in the vicarage—their idyllic repast only to be interrupted by murder most foul. Heavens, what on earth were they burning? The smoke had such a strange acrid tang, and it was getting stronger. She heard footsteps behind her and half-turned to find the headmaster practically on her heels.

"Dr. Woodbury! Good afternoon."

"Hello, Laura. Do you smell something burning?"

"I'd been wondering about that myself. At first, I thought it was just someone's fireplace—we're not far from the faculty housing, after all. But it's too sharp for firewood, don't you think?"

They both quickened their pace, concerned now. They rounded the corner of the upper school library quad and the smell was much stronger now. Dr. Woodbury charged across the driveway and through the library doors. Laura shaded her eyes against the low winter sun as she walked around the building. She soon spotted corkscrews of smoke curling under the eaves on the west side. She called 911 on her cell phone as she made for the building entrance, only to step aside for a stream of exiting faculty and students.

"Form groups of your home rooms," one of the librarians yelled. "No running!"

The students walked as fast as they could without actually running and gathered in assorted chattering clusters. Four groups, three librarians and two faculty. Good. Laura walked over to the smallest group of seven students.

"You are not here for a class, I take it?" she asked.

"No, Miss Jones," said a podgy spotty tenth grader. "Just doing some research for a paper."

"If you came with someone, or sat near someone, are they here now?"

"Oh, God," he said, looking around. "Maggie's not out here." He craned his neck to look over at the other groups. "She went upstairs to look for something in the archives."

"You mean Maggie Brandt?" Laura asked. He nodded, frantic and immobilized.

A window in the upper level blew out and flames lashed the side wall like angry tongues. The one next to it followed, adding to the sharp debris strewn below. Where was Dr. Woodbury? No one had come out of the building for at least five minutes. The adrenaline-producing screams of fire engines drew closer. Laura ran back to the building. He must be in trouble. She heard the sounds of trucks' brakes and men's shouts only vaguely as she pushed through the doorway. The smoke had seeped down here, too. She headed for the stairs just as Dr. Woodbury appeared through the haze with a girl over his shoulder. He started down, clutching the rail with one hand, clearly in pain. Laura ran to him.

"Get out," he rasped. "The fire's spreading."

"I'm not leaving you," she said. "You're hurt."

Two firemen reached them and one took the girl as the other told Dr. Woodbury to lean on him. Laura supported his other side, and they all emerged into the chilly air to the applause of the onlookers. Maggie was already being loaded into the ambulance.

"You too, sir," said the fire chief.

"No, no, I'll be fine."

"No, sir, you have burns and probably smoke inhalation. We'll have a look at them on the way. "

"Focus your attention on the girl."

"She'll be fine. Same as you, minor burns and smoke inhalation. In you get, sir." His tone was firm.

"Listen to him, Dr. Woodbury. Go and let the doctors have a look at you," Laura said. He looked her in the face for a long few seconds and she wondered if he saw her feelings for him reflected in her eyes.

"Alert Tina. I guess that's why we have deputies," he said with a limp smile before limping reluctantly to the ambulance. He turned back. "And, thank you."

Laura watched the ambulance pull away before making for the administration building. He was due another dinner. And he wouldn't get away so easily this time. What a guy!

20

S he shivered from nerves and cold. He'd been in the store yet again that afternoon, quite annoyed he hadn't heard from her. She apologized profusely, explaining that someone threw out the paper he'd written his address on before she could put it somewhere safe. He wrote it out again. He hadn't spent long browsing, bought a used book about the founding of Toronto, and remarked he had to hurry off to the florist before they closed.

"I'm going to a dinner party at seven this evening, a nice walk through the park, you know."

"Well, wrap up warmly. These spring evenings can be quite chilly."

"Yes, thank you, I will," he said, mollified. "See you soon!"

It was already half past. The green front door opened and there he was, picked out by the hall light, a red muffler wrapped around his neck. He strode across the street and into the park. It seemed deathly quiet as she followed, keeping to the trees off the path, alternately tiptoeing and mincing like a poodle in an effort not to shuffle the dead leaves blown into little heaps by the wind. He stopped suddenly, looking around him with his nose in the air like a deer sensing a hunter. Lily tried to hold her breath, but her fear was too urgent to be deprived of air. She'd never felt like this before—only alert and focused, determined to rid herself of a problem. Where was that anticipation, that piquant feeling of dangerous adventure? Was she out of practice? Perhaps not so much a question of practice, rather that she knew what awaited her if she made another mistake. Before, she'd fixated on losing the trappings and privilege of her affluent life. What she'd lost were her children, her freedom, and her dignity. She'd gotten it all wrong. And she certainly understood what she had to lose now. Friends, small pleasures. And maybe she could somehow get back into her children's lives. Toby was a loose end, though.

He was on the move again. *Softly, softly*. She felt for the knife in her pocket and gasped when she clutched the blade instead of the hilt. She flattened herself behind an old oak, its vast trunk big enough to hide three. She wrapped her scarf around her bleeding palm and risked edging around the tree to see what Toby was doing. He was still walking, but slower now. He had not registered her presence. Unless he was faking it, suspected a mugger. More and more of those in Toronto these days. She started walking again, keeping farther back than before.

What was he up to? His head had sunk between his shoulders, his pace slowing even more. He flopped down onto a bench, wedging himself into a corner, his back to Lily. Strange place to sit on a chilly night. Maybe a trap? She inched closer, moving behind each tree that lined the path until she was close enough to see him clearly under the streetlight near the bench. His chin almost touched his chest as his shoulders heaved. "Samantha," he whispered. "Samantha. Why did it have to be you?" He sobbed some more.

Lily moved up behind him, catlike. She stood at the corner of the bench behind him, her sliced hand aching where she gripped the knife, outside her pocket now. He didn't seem to have heard her approach. It would be over in minutes. "No man ever loved a woman the way I loved you," he murmured.

Lily had tried to suppress all those memories, but they swarmed her mind now like ants on a dunghill. Victor had loved her. Until near the end. Would he have sobbed for her this way? The old Victor would have. For sure. She saw Samantha's sprawling body after she'd smashed the woman's head on the garage floor, then Toby's grief-stricken face in the weeks and months after. These things had meant nothing to her then. She'd thought herself so smart, so superior to all of them.

What she remembered most was all those eyes on her, always watching, even in her dreams. She'd sensed them fixed on her at the trial, all her former friends trying to find some sort of clue in her face, asking themselves how they could have missed the evil. Because that's what they thought her. Evil. But she wasn't really. Not anymore. Although here she stood, knife in hand. She'd known better than to look into the eyes of predators in that skanky prison as they watched and waited for their opportunity, or the patients waiting and waiting for anything at all in that voodoo hospital. Her hand trembled and her grip loosened. The knife dropped, clanging as it hit a pebble. Toby whipped around.

"What do you want?" His voice, choky and furious, lacked the fear she might have expected.

"It's Lily, from the bookshop. I often walk this way in the evening. Are you all right?"

"Yes, of course. Just taking a short break on my way to my friend's house. Will you walk with me?"

"If you want."

They walked slowly, in silence. *The killing is over. I'm a different person now, and besides, I mustn't draw attention to myself. Peter was different—a predator of the worst kind. Putting him out of commission was a social service. I draw the line. I do.*

"Good night, Lily. Thanks for keeping me company. I hit a low spot. I miss my wife terribly sometimes."

"It was my pleasure, Toby. I wasn't much company, though. I didn't say a word."

"Just having someone next to you is worth a lot some-times, you know."

"I know. Good night."

"When can I see you without your bandages?"

"Very soon, Toby, very soon."

Lily trudged home, a couple of miles or more and she felt exhausted.

She couldn't sleep. The one time she'd dropped off she'd had terrible dreams about being chased round a table by Samantha, whose open head wound dripped blood and brains. She had to write, had to write a different part of the story, a calm piece.

"Dr. Woodbury!"

"Well, we certainly run into each other in strange places."

Laura had flopped into her seat somewhat out of breath as she'd been running late. She loved chamber music, and shouldn't have been surprised that he did.

"Have you heard this group before?" he asked. His eyes—blue or gray? Hard to tell in this light. She could lose herself in them. How trite, get a grip!

"Yes, they play here every couple of months and they sound better every time. The cellist was a Mackie student, you know." Was she babbling?

"Oh, that's good to know. Maybe we should go backstage after the concert. What do you think?"

"I always do. They all go over the road to McKeever's afterward for a beer or two." She took a deep breath. "Why don't you join us? I think the bar runs to other things if you don't like beer."

"You know, I think I will." The lights dimmed, and he turned to face the stage as did she. Her chest felt fluttery. "I do like a nice cold beer from time to time."

21

She'd have to disappear again soon. Seattle? Maybe she should take a trip there and scout around. Lily went up to her bedroom and unlocked her desk. Her Lily passport had been the last of her stash, so she'd have to get creative again. She opened it up to the photo. Perhaps no longer a good likeness. She hoped it wouldn't cause problems. She'd better ask her surgeon for a letter. They might tell her to get a new passport. This one was good until … shit! That little crook had promised her a full five years. How could she not have checked it? Feeling everything closing on her had made her sloppy. If only they'd all left her alone. Stupid thinking; how could they? No choice now. She'd have to fly down to the city and get a new one. A couple of new ones. Depended on the price, and she'd need a Canadian visa for the Lily one.

She grabbed her coin purse and walked to her neighborhood phone booth, dialing the number from memory. "Ned is no longer with us," said an unctuous voice on the other end after all the coins had dropped.

"My name is Iris Hall. I need a couple of new books plus a Canadian bookmark in one. And a calling card. How soon can you do them?" Papers rustled. Did they actually keep records? Risky. No, they wouldn't know the name Iris.

"Yes, here you are, Iris. When can you come in?"

"Monday morning."

"Noon Monday. $1,500 for a week's turnaround, $2,500 for a day. Cash, of course."

"My, that's a big jump. And Ned cheated me last time. He promised me five years, and he made it for only three."

"The market sets the prices, lady. But yes, Ned sometimes cut corners. That's why he is no longer with us. In any sense."

"I see." Lily's skin crawled. "I need the express option. See you Monday at noon."

Well, poor old Ned. She'd relied on him for years. The sleazy, fat slob had been her security backup. But he shouldn't have cheated her like that. He must have known not all his clients would take a scam lightly.

Lily made her reservations for the flight and a little hotel she remembered downtown, not so far from the dealer's office that hid in the rear of an artists' supply store. What would she buy this time? A sketch pad and a set of pencils, maybe. She should take art lessons and see if she was any good. Good thing she'd held onto all those American dollars. It's not as if she had a credit card, after all. She must call Magaly.

"Hello, Magaly. How are you?"

"Well, only so-so. I can't seem to catch my breath." She coughed. "That cold just lingered. The cough never went away."

"Oh, Magaly. I'm so sorry. What does the doctor say?"

"I had a whole lot of tests yesterday. I see him again Monday." Magaly's gasps pushed harshly down the line.

"Why ever didn't you call me? I would have come with you."

"I know, Lily, but I didn't want to make a big deal. Hilda, you know, she worries too much. And the doctor said she has a little heart problem."

"What! Why all the secrecy? You mustn't keep these things from me. When you need help, you should know better than to be too proud to ask. Do you think I'll find it a burden, an imposition? Never!" Anxiety rocked her already seething mind.

A silent minute, then a little sob. "Oh, Lily, you are so precious to us, you know. Like a daughter."

Lily felt close to tears herself. "Magaly, I have to fly down to New York on Sunday to attend to some business. As soon as I get back, probably Wednesday, I'll come over. I'll be thinking of you."

"See you Wednesday, Lily. Bye."

Canadian doctors didn't order tests unless they were worried. So, maybe they were both sick. And both in their seventies. Hell and damnation! She hadn't been to see them for a couple of weeks. Unforgivable. You can't do that with old people.

Wendy! She'd better think up a good excuse.

On Sunday afternoon, Lily held her carefully folded surgeon's letter in her hand as she lined up at American immigration. She was glad you had to do this in the Toronto airport when you flew to the US. The suspense would be over sooner.

The middle-aged officer looked bored. "My picture is not a very good likeness. I suffered burns in a house fire. I have a letter from my surgeon here."

He scanned the letter, stared at her for a couple of minutes, then down at her photo. "Well, little lady, glad you came through it. Tell him from me he does great work!"

"Good, so you can see it's me, then."

"Not if you hadn't pointed it out. But face shape, eyes. Yup! How long have you been in Canada?"

"Twenty years."

"In Toronto?"

"No, only a couple of years. I lived in Manitoba before my husband died."

"Have a nice day, ma'am."

"Thank you." And she walked through customs without a hitch. Face shape? Another new hairdo. Eyes? Glasses. Which she'd sometimes thought she might need lately. She had until noon tomorrow when the passport guy would take her photo. She could have her eyes checked at one of those walk-in places. They did it all in a couple of hours. A wig. She'd let her hair grow. After singeing so much of it in the fire, she'd had to have it cut really short when she got out of the hospital and it was still too short. Short hair revealed a great deal. Yes, it would have to be a wig. She knew where to go—it wouldn't be the first time.

She managed to get the last of the cabs in line at La Guardia and felt as if she were passing through a foreign country as they made the long trek down to lower Manhattan.

This didn't look like her town. Of course, it hadn't been for years, and that part of her youth spent in New York hadn't been great. Lily/Rose/Pansy had traveled several worlds away from that life.

The hotel looked smaller and seedier than she remembered. She hoped it was clean. The streaked-blonde receptionist was perkily polite, which was somewhat reassuring. The elevator was fairly new, so the place must still be going strong. As she opened the door to her room, she expected to see the same prints that had always greeted her in the old days, pictures she associated with change and escape: the Manhattan skyline, the Empire State Building, and the Statue of Liberty reaching for the heavens, and other such New York icons. Flowers now, pictures of flowers flagrantly opening themselves to the viewer. She'd seen them before, but not here, and she somehow felt let down.

Lily unpacked her toiletries and used a wipe on her face to get off the city grime that could give you acne if you didn't keep on top of it. She touched up her lipstick and thought she'd scope out the shop and find a bite to eat. Then an early night, since she had to make an early start.

The shop looked about the same. She peered at the items in the window; quite a lot of new types of artist's materials, fancy handmade paper, too. She might get some of that to wrap a nice gift for Hilda and Magaly. Expensive chocolates, perhaps. Should someone with a heart condition eat chocolate? No harm in one now and again, surely. Hilda was always going on about English chocolate being even better than Swiss, so she'd look for some. Although, English chocolates were probably easier to find in Toronto than in New York. The Commonwealth and all that.

A light went on in the back of the shop. Someone moving back and forth, no more than a shadow, a small, thin shadow. A door slammed in the light. Working late.

Lily walked on. There wasn't too much choice in this area, as most of the small number of restaurants only opened for the lunch crowd. Here was one, Indian. One of those holes in the wall that often had the best home-cooked food. She opened the door and looked around. She felt quite out of place in this gathering of Indian families for a moment, but that kind of clientele was a good sign. She chose a dal platter with lassi and papadums. She always found lentils satisfyingly filling, and the platter had five little dishes with dal prepared in different ways. The lassi soothed her throat after a particularly spicy spoonful. They'd added fresh mint to the yoghurt drink, delicious and refreshing. She broke one of her peppered papadums, the Indian answer to chips. Lily began to relax. She hadn't had Indian food in ages. She never thought about seeking it out, but she should eat it more often, especially as she ate less and less meat these days. It often made her feel nauseated.

Lily fingered some of the papers. A young man had been hovering for some time. "Can I help you?" he finally asked.

"I'm having a hard time making up my mind," she answered, pointing to two ivory sheets, one with an Iris embedded in the rag and the other with what looked like anemones. "You have so many interesting things this week."

"I think the Iris would be more to your taste," he said quietly.

"You are very perceptive. Is he available?"

"Of course, madam. I will put this in a bag for you and bring it to the back. Go carefully."

A couple of young women seemed focused on a starter paint set. "For my little niece," one of them explained. "Her birthday's on Saturday." The young man steered them farther to the front window area to show them something else, leaving Lily free to edge her way to the door that announced the back room private, for staff only.

"Good morning. Mrs. Hall is it?" He rose to his feet, or rather unfolded. She looked up at him. His face, all bones and angles, strangely blank.

"Good morning. I didn't catch your name when I called."

"I didn't provide one. You can call me Mr. Oliver."

"Very well, Mr. Oliver. Shall we proceed?"

"Remove your coat. I believe you chose the $2,500 option, Mrs. Hall?"

"Excuse me, please." She turned to the wall while she unzipped the front of her pants and pulled out the fat bag that curved around her hip. She zipped up again and handed it to him. "I'd like the bag back, please."

He retrieved the wad and handed back the bag before counting the $100 bills. "Very well, let's get started. Fill out this form first, please. You'll get it back with your passports."

"And the Social Security card."

"Of course."

Lily filled in the legend for her passports and had her picture taken. She felt uneasy with this man. He said nothing beyond necessary instructions.

"Where can I reach you, Mrs. Hall?"

"I won't be reachable for the next twenty-four hours. Just tell me when to come back."

His eyes flickered annoyance. "Noon tomorrow."

"Very well."

He opened a panel in the door and peered out. "The way is clear. Go now."

Lily walked toward the front desk, realizing the young man hadn't brought the paper back to her. She looked around and jumped when he popped up from the counter beside the till.

"That will be $3.65 with tax, madam."

"Really? This place has become expensive."

"Yes, it has, hasn't it, madam, still, you get what you pay for, I always say."

Cheeky little sod. For twenty-five hundred buckos, they should have thrown in the paper. Still, they had to make it look good. You never knew who was watching. She'd better dodge around a bit. She'd take a cab to midtown and look at the shops. Lunch and English chocolate.

Lily wore her reversible raincoat the next morning and took a tortuous route to the shop, arriving about fifteen minutes early. There were a lot of customers today. Ned had been smart, making sure the shelves at the back had very little of general interest in them, and Mr. Oliver had kept it that way. He used the space to store stacks of chipped frames, cans of paint and thinner, and old model kits, so the customers mainly stayed up front. She picked up a dusty kit for some battleship and studied the picture. She wasn't used to her new glasses yet.

"You can go in now." That young man moved like a cat. She slipped through the door.

"Ah, Mrs. Hall."

"Mr. Oliver. May I see them?"

"Of course." His gloved hand placed them gently in front of her. Lily sat and read all the data carefully, especially the expiration date. "All original? No numbers from dead people?"

"Of course not. I am a consummate professional." His voice was curt and angry; he glared down at her. What a strange accent. Almost British, but not quite.

"I'm sorry. It's just that I dealt with poor Ned for so long."

"Poor Ned got greedy. I worked with him for a couple of years, you know."

"Did you? What happened to him?"

"An after-hours robbery gone wrong. At least that's the official version." He sat opposite her.

Lily looked at him again. His face had cracked a smile, and it wasn't pretty. Chapped lips and gray teeth like old tombstones.

"Now, Mrs. Hall, I need to know where you can be reached."

"Why? If I need you again, I will call."

"It is my policy." His hand closed over the passports and he rose to his full height, clutching them to his heart. "Be sensible, my dear. I have something you want. And maybe you have something I want. I need a little insurance."

"Your so-called policy is very bad for business. Where will you find your clients when word gets out?"

"Most of my clients don't know each other, or even other people who would need my services."

"How do you think I found Ned? Word of mouth."

"There are customers, and then there are other customers. You will never tell anyone about my services."

"Are we talking about blackmail?"

"How you jump to conclusions, my dear. No, I just need to know where to find you. And no lying, I have ways of finding people."

Lily's breath came in shallow bursts now. He smiled again, mistaking her expression for fear. "I'll write it down." Pansy's name and one of her old addresses.

"Goodbye, Mr. Oliver."

"It's been a pleasure." Not for her.

Lily grabbed her passports and left the room, almost forgetting to be discrete. She had as much to lose as him. More now. She'd always been able to trust old Ned.

She walked south, turning sudden corners, stopping to look in shop windows. There he was. She'd spotted him waiting outside the shop. She walked into a small hotel that advertised lunch and found a seat. She ordered, then slipped into the ladies' room where she turned her raincoat to the solid black side, removed her wig, and put her glasses away. She walked through the lobby and out, earning only a cursory glance from the threadbare character who'd followed her. She took a cab to her hotel. She didn't check out, but packed her few belongings and caught another cab uptown. Another third-rate hotel that took cash without ID, this time on 57th. Thank God she could remove her coat. May in New York was warmer than in Toronto.

Lily kicked off her shoes, pulled back the coverlet, and lay on her back, thinking. It wouldn't be easy. Who knew what connections Mr. Oliver might have? He carried the air of a powerful man and looked like a shoo-in for the role of Professor Moriarty. For sure, he'd been the one to kill old Ned. He'd be looking for her, assuming she'd be easy pickings. This might take a while. It had to happen quickly or she wouldn't make her flight tomorrow. She had nothing with her. Fire was the only thing. He worked at night. Fire at the back door, fire at the front. Was there a window at back? Yes, she'd seen a curtain. But it was most likely barred. Lily felt a little knot in her stomach. This was different. Mr. Oliver was bad, a predator. She'd have to wear the wig and glasses since she'd be traveling without and she'd better look different. Where could she get gasoline near the hotel? She'd use a couple of the pillowcases and towels and soak them in it. It would look odd if she asked for a gas station—a guest without a car. *Okay, get going.*

Lily opened her case and managed to cram in the linens. She grabbed a couple of newspapers from the lobby and walked out of the hotel, hoping no one would question her, although she'd paid in advance. She bought a large bottle of distilled water at the corner drugstore (she would empty it and fill it with gasoline, if she ever found any), then stopped at a nearby convenience store for matches. She suddenly noticed several large bags on a lower shelf in the back corner. Charcoal. And three containers of barbeque starter. What an odd thing to find in the middle of Manhattan. That would do as well as gasoline, so she put all three in her basket and gratefully left the heavy bottle of water in the corner. *My brother's giving a barbecue in Queens*, she'd say, but the clerk couldn't care less about her business, immersed as he was in an impassioned call to his girlfriend.

Another cab took her to her first hotel, where she went up to her room, only to find herself locked out. Damn, key cards were a nuisance! The housekeeping staff must have surmised she'd left. Well, there was no one around, and all she had to do was take off her wig. It would have been nice to lie down until dark, though, and be able to comb her hair properly rather than raking through it with her fingers. There must be a ladies' room on the ground floor. No, too conspicuous with her case.

She strolled outside and hailed yet another cab to take her to a café a couple of blocks away from Mr. Oliver's place. How could she be sure he was there? She'd just have to assume if she saw a light on. He'd be unlikely to trust anyone else alone in there at night.

The carrot-ginger soup and veggie sandwich had been great and, invigorated, Lily was glad to find her nerve still held. This wasn't about hurting decent people. And this man would hurt her if he could, ruin her life if he didn't actually set someone on her. Time to go. The shops had closed, and it looked quite dark now. No rain, thank goodness, that would have ruined everything. She walked toward the store and turned onto the street behind. No entry there. There must be an alleyway. *Quiet and careful, he might enter or exit that way.* Her nose found the trashcans, and they were big enough to hide between in the dark. Thank God for the city's war on rats. Lily hunkered down just to the right of the back door. There was the window, barred as expected, a bright light shining behind the curtain. She could just make out a moving figure. He might have a client with him like he obviously had the other night, but she couldn't help that. She pulled the stuff out of the case and risked getting up to spread the linens over the cans. She soaked them in starter fluid. The gases stung her throat and nostrils. The door opened a little and she shrank back down. The smell was strong. Would he notice?

"Good night, Mr. Oliver. And thank you." A young woman's voice, sounded educated.

"Good night, my dear. I'll call you next week to make sure everything went well."

"Oh, you are a dear man." Breathy now. Silly cow, he'd call and nothing would be all right ever again. Lily would solve more problems than her own tonight.

The woman came out quickly and looked around before scurrying away, obviously too nervous in a New York alley in the dark to pay attention to strange odors. Mr. Oliver stayed put. Lily took some towels quickly to the front of the store and laid them at the door, making sure no one was around. She set them alight, and they blazed almost at once. She rushed round to the back and did the same thing at the back door after squirting fluid on the door and window frame and siding. No solid brownstone buildings down here; cheap wood construction, old and dry.

Lily picked up her suitcase and left. She couldn't afford to wait to see the results. She walked slowly along a couple of side streets until she found herself on Broadway, where she trudged for what seemed like ten blocks before finding a cab to take her to the hotel and bed. She arrived back in her room and, surprisingly, found it was only ten. She took a shower and turned on the TV. A sitcom about young couples whose lives seemed to swing hopelessly between love interests of one sort or another, then the news. Nothing yet.

Then, fifteen minutes in, "*...We have breaking news...*"

And there was the store, blackened and twisted, and those on either side didn't look so good. All that paint and thinner conveniently near the back, great fuel. But did he get out?

"*We have just heard that a body has been found and is thought to be that of the owner.*"

Yes! Lily bounced up and down in her bed like a birthday child.

"*...no sprinkler system. The fire is thought to be arson. Their spokesman declined to comment when asked if this could be linked to the Chelsea arsonist.*"

Well, what luck, she wasn't the only arsonist in town! She could go home with a light heart.

As she drifted into sleep, she thought about her old landlady, similarly incinerated. What had happened to the new Lily? Nothing, still trudging down the road to redemption.

22

Lily passed through to the departure lounge and found a seat. There was still an hour to go until boarding. She looked at her watch: only eleven, but she fancied a glass of wine. She walked over to the bar and found a seat near a group of five or six young men, all carrying briefcases and all dressed like ambitious young corporate types. As she sipped on her merlot, she listened in. Lawyers.

"You know Simon's leaving at the end of the month?" said one.

"Yeah, he's a dark horse, isn't he? I never knew he was interviewing. Did you, Bob? Oh, here he is now. Hi, there, come and sit down." Chair legs dragged across the tough carpet.

"Hello everyone. How's it going?" Andrew. Lily sat almost paralyzed, sick, unable to turn.

"We were just talking about you. Moving on, are you?"

"Yes, I kind of miss the East Coast."

"Oh, want to be a fast-track New Yorker, do you?"

"No, I'm transferring to the Charlotte, North Carolina, office."

"Why in hell would anyone want to bury themselves down there?"

"My wife is from there, and I like it, actually. Like the people, too." Her Andrew had a wife. *Married.*

"Well, you're a saint, kiddo, sacrificing your career like that for the wife."

"For the baby, too, so he can get to know his grandparents. It'll be great having family around. Anne feels a bit isolated in Seattle. And it's no sacrifice. I learned what's really important in life a long time ago." Yes, poor boy, he'd learned the hard way. The baby! *I'm a grandmother.* She turned, slowly, and looked. She couldn't bear not to. He looked thinner, still solemn, seemed content. She stared. She shouldn't, but she had to. Had to absorb his face, his voice—savor it, hoard it. Their eyes met, and he stiffened, his mouth opened. *God, no, he mustn't,* and then his shoulders relaxed, and he looked away quickly, as did she.

"That's our flight being called. Time to go," Andrew said. His voice sounded a little shaky. Had he thought he recognized her for a moment? Her bearing, the shape of her face? She listened to the busy rustling and chair scraping and knocking of bags against chairs as they left. Andrew was gone. Lily rushed out into the ladies' room, excused herself as she pushed past a couple of women waiting, and darted into the just-vacated stall. She vomited her wine, her bile, her grief. She leaned back against the door sweating, waves of dizziness almost making her sink to the floor. Only the realization of the probable state of the floor kept her upright, her breath coming in wheezing gulps.

She had to catch her flight. It must be nearly time. She unlocked the door and went to wash her hands and splash her face with cold water.

"Are you all right?" a timid voice asked.

"Yes, quite all right now, thank you." She caught sight of her bag, which she'd quite forgotten after she tossed it against the bathroom wall as she rushed in. Amazing it hadn't been stolen. She picked it up and walked quickly to the departure gate. The line had almost gone through, but she saw the usual backup as people fought their bags into the overhead compartments.

Please, no more complications. She didn't have the energy she used to. She'd be sixty in a couple of years, even though that's not what her passport said; she'd earned a little concession to vanity.

She must compose herself. As soon as the seatbelt sign was turned off, she hauled a notebook and pen out of her tote and pulled down her tray. She began to write almost feverishly.

> Only four weeks until Christmas. Laura thought she'd ask her cousin Andy to come to her place for a change. He still lived in the family home, and that probably contributed to his depression. She would see if Gary were free, although perhaps he had relatives he wanted to see.
>
> She'd rattled the whole family their last Christmas together. Her mother had invited her brother Alan's new family, to Laura's disgust. His new wife and her two girls, Lexie and Justine, seemed pleasant enough. Her uncle insisted on an extra

helping of pie for Justine, and almost simpered over her, although the girl murmured she didn't want any and riveted her eyes on her plate.

"So, you've started on her, now, have you?" Laura blurted out, revolted. The room's buzz curled into a silent question mark.

Her mother turned her ashen face to Laura and hissed, "Be quiet at once!"

The new wife, her pallor even more pronounced, shot up and ran from the room. "See what you've done now, you wicked girl!" said her mother.

Laura looked at her uncle. "You are a rotten pervert. I cannot sit by and let you ruin her life like you ruined mine."

The man's face took on a dangerous purple hue. "I don't know what you are talking about. Your mother is right. You are a wicked girl."

"No, she isn't," whispered the young girl across the table to Lily. She turned to her stepfather. "You do nasty things to me. You are the wicked one."

Laura's father, always one to shrink from confrontation, finally came through. He'd been staring, unbelieving, at his brother-in-law and now swiveled to face his daughter. "Laura, did he molest you?"

"Yes, he did. Every summer when I went to stay with them, nearly every day."

"My God, why didn't you tell us, Laura?"

"I tried to tell Mom. She wouldn't believe me."

"Is that so?" he asked his wife.

"Darling, how could you possibly believe this nonsense, and you know how—"

"Alan, get out and don't ever come back. And you can leave the girls with us until I have spoken to their mother and sorted this out."

Her mother had never forgiven Laura or her husband. But Laura had exaggerated a little. Uncle Alan had not ruined her life. She'd finally come to realize that it hadn't been her fault. She had made a success of her life and fallen in love with a wonderful man. She would live happily ever after. She would.

Why did this keep creeping in? Why not? It was something from her own life modified for Laura. Perhaps that's what most writers do. Although, not all those writers of mysteries and thrillers could possibly have experienced all those traumas. Reading about them, perhaps in the newspapers and in other novels, would provide the right fodder. She'd learned about romance from other novels, after all. And this passage definitely packed a punch. She felt quite pleased with herself.

Toronto—what a relief to see the lake as they came in to land. She'd grown attached to the place. It seemed a kinder city than New York.

"You know your passport expires soon, ma'am?"

"Yes, as soon as I get home, I'm going to get it renewed."

"What were you doing in the United States?"

"Visiting friends."

"Have a nice day, ma'am."

Another hurdle overcome.

It felt good to be home. Lily dropped her small case by the front door and sank into her recliner. Yes, good to be home. Wonderful feeling, and it had nothing to do with nice furniture. Part of the wonderful feeling came from seeing Andrew. Her Andrew married and a father! And he'd be a wonderful husband and father. She knew that for sure. She must call Magaly to ask about the tests. Later. It was only three and the two of them would be arguing about tea or coffee with their cake. Magaly would brew coffee and Hilda a pot of tea. Lily couldn't figure out why they just didn't do what they wanted to do in the first place without exhaustive debate. Little things were so important in their world and never put to rest.

23

Hilda and Magaly sat next to each other on Hilda's chintz-covered sofa, holding each other and rocking as Hilda cried a pool of tears into Magaly's sweater. Magaly felt even more sorry for her than she did for herself. Death would come for her soon, and not quietly. Unless she decided otherwise.

"Now, now, Hilda, this is not good for your heart, you know that."

"I can't help it, Magaly. I'm so scared. I might have to have an operation, a terrible one, and you are so sick. Why aren't you having an operation? They must be able to do something."

"No, they cannot. We'll try some chemotherapy and radiation, but they do not hope for much. It is stage four, Hilda. That means the cancer has traveled to other places."

"I can't bear life without my best friend. And you don't even sound scared."

"Of course, I am scared, Hilda. Scared of pain and losing my dignity and my mind and losing my chance to do so many things. I wanted to go back to Hungary, just to see how it is after sixty years. I never said, but I wanted to do it. I could not really afford it, but I might have found a way."

This led to another bout of weeping and Magaly joined in this time. After a while, they pulled back. "I'm going to wash my face," said Hilda. "Then I'll make you some coffee."

"No, no Hilda, I make my own coffee. You never got the hang of it!"

"All right, then, I'll make a pot of tea. I know how to do that rather well," Hilda retorted with a sniff as she marched out, embarrassed by her emotional outburst.

Magaly leaned back and hugged a cushion. So, this was how it was to end. All those years of struggle. The children, how would they behave once they found out? Hilda and she had already willed their share of the condo to each other, and Lily would inherit from the survivor. The children would be furious. But Lily could handle it. She hoped Lily would care for Hilda. Hilda would need care and constant reassurance. Did she have the patience? Probably so.

A couple of hours later, Magaly had found a bottle of sherry and they were each on their second glass.

"Is this good for us?" asked Hilda, not sounding much concerned.

"You bet it is!" said Magaly, punching the air and grinning. Her face dimmed as the phone rang. "Lily. She was due back today."

"Yes, I know. Should we tell her?" Hilda's eyes brimmed again.

"We have to. I'll do it." Magaly stiffened herself and went over to the phone.

"Hello, Lily. No, not so good, not so good." As she went on talking, she heard Hilda begin to sob again. "She's coming over," Magaly said as she put down the phone. "Pull yourself together, for God's sake. We must be brave for Lily's sake." She knew Hilda didn't fully understand the gravity of her own condition, although she was very afraid of the bypass. And she would not be able to handle Magaly's decline. Well, when things got to a certain point, Magaly would put an end to it. She'd get pills. They always gave you plenty of pain pills. And she could complain about not being able to sleep. Plenty of pills, that would do the trick, then a lovely long pain-free sleep.

Magaly and Hilda sat and waited. Hilda nodded off thanks to her unaccustomed indulgence in two glasses of sherry, only to awaken with a jolt when the doorbell rang.

Lily tossed and turned, then stared at the street lamp's amber reflection on the ceiling. Her two aunties ill, one of them terminal. She had some idea about what Magaly would have to go through from newspaper articles she'd read. Maybe she'd ease her out when the time came. No, not her call. That would have to be Magaly's decision. But she wouldn't shrink from it. From the sound of it, that time would come sooner rather than later.

Funny how a cold fish like her could be so devastated by the prospect of losing these two. Their expressions while Magaly broke the news haunted her. Hilda, lips quivering, eyes pink, trying so desperately to be brave, while Magaly's voice had turned cold and clinical, warding off pity as if brandishing garlic at a vampire.

She planned to move near Andrew, but that would have to wait. Magaly and Hilda needed her. And she needed them. Unless Hilda's health took a sudden turn for the worse, Magaly would go first and Hilda would have to be taken care of. Her children were useless, and she had to be protected from them to some extent, too. She'd better buy a car because she'd have to go every day, even though the building offered some services; but if they got bad, they'd try to institutionalize them. Not if Lily could help it. Oh, damn, she'd have to take a road test and all that. Well, it had to be done.

She'd keep track of Andrew on the internet. He'd be staying with the same firm, so it shouldn't be a problem. Strange she hadn't looked for her other two children, Lucy and Justin. Well she would, she'd find them, too.

Oh, those poor old girls. It shouldn't happen like this. They should have had several more years of good times. The tears came, then, and she wept into her pillow as she hadn't done since she was a young fourteen-year-old who had just smothered her baby sister. A good deed, but a heavy burden and, she realized now, a burden that had twisted her in some way. A mercy killing to save that little one from a lifetime of pain and degradation. She wasn't a monster, not really, not anymore. She'd always had a good reason for what she did. And now she'd found two dear old aunties, she was going to lose them.

The next few years would be hard. So hard. Then, off to Andrew. If she could get away for a week, she'd think about going down to Charlotte and buying a house once she'd found out where he was living. She could always rent it out. She had something to look forward to, and that eased her mind.

For now, she had a duty to someone other than herself. What a turn-up for the books for this loner. She might have to quit Wendy's soon. She'd be sorry about that. Another group of people she cared about. If it weren't for Andrew, she'd stay. She should befriend Natasha. She'd like to know more about her story, anyway. If she felt the girl would stick around and was honest, she might suggest to Wendy that she'd be a good one to train as a bookkeeper. Nancy was coming back, but only part-time, wanting to be home when Ellie got back from school. Lily certainly didn't want to leave Wendy in the lurch.

First and foremost she was a mother. And a grandmother. She must get to know that child. She'd love him. Definitely.

24

The next year was so depressing that Lily didn't know if her constant exhaustion arose from grief or nursing. Her house didn't have enough downstairs space to install beds for Hilda and Magaly, so she thought it best to take care of them in their condo. She bought a small used car, which she could park in her driveway and their allotted parking space. It saved a lot of time. Of course, she had to resign from the bookshop.

Hilda could manage breakfast for now, so Lily went to them at around noon to prepare a sandwich for lunch and stayed to cook dinner and help with more as they went downhill. Magaly had decided that the treatments available to her would only ruin her last months rather than postpone the inevitable for any significant period of time. Hospice took over when she became too weak and breathless to manage on her own. Lily could tell she suffered a lot of pain, too, although the old lady never complained. Lily suspected she was hoarding her pills. Hospice suggested moving Magaly to a hospice center, given Hilda's frail condition, but they both protested vehemently. They needed every moment together they could hold on to.

Hilda spent most of her time by Magaly's bed reading to her or reliving some of their memories. She could see the toll it was taking on Hilda. She practically had to drag her away to the doctor for her own appointments. Her doctor wasn't happy with her lack of progress and cautioned her to avoid stress. There was no way to do that under the circumstances.

One evening while Hilda was sleeping in front of the TV, Lily sat reading by Magaly, who was dozing herself. The hospice nurse had administered her painkillers a couple of hours before.

"Lily." The raspy voice startled her.

"Yes, Magaly, what can I get you?

"Drawer. Other side. Pills. I need them. All of them." She coughed and coughed, before finally falling back, spent. She panted and fought for breath.

Lily went around to the bedside table and rummaged around. There they were, wrapped in aluminum foil. About ten of them. Opiates.

"Magaly." No response. "Magaly, can you hear me?"

The old lady, once heavy set and robust, looked as if she had folded in on herself. Her eyes fluttered open. "Give me."

"Listen to me. If I give you more than two, your stomach will reject them. I'll give you two now, then another two in a couple of hours, and again until they are all gone."

"Yes. Love you. You are my daughter."

Lily started to cry. She couldn't stop herself. She popped one pill in Magaly's mouth and held her head while she swallowed it down with water. She waited a minute before doing it again. She put the rest of the pills into her pocket and kissed Magaly's forehead. Magaly pursed her lips a little and made a kissing sound.

Lily sat down and stared at the woman who should have been her mother, or at least her aunt. Everyone left in the end. She tried to go back to her book, but couldn't focus. Would they do an autopsy? Probably not. Magaly was under hospice care, after all, and was terminally ill.

Lily went out to Hilda, who had just awoken and looked around, confused.

"Hilda, you woke up! What were you watching?"

"Oh, can't remember now."

"Would you like some cocoa? We can probably find something nice to watch."

"Oh, thank you, Lily. You are so good to us. I wish I'd had a daughter like you."

"And how I wish I'd had a mother like you, Hilda."

"Wasn't your mother very nice?"

"No. Both my parents were drunks, and my home life was very unpleasant. You and Magaly are my family now."

"Oh, Lily. Not for long, though. What will you do after we've gone?" Hilda twisted her ever-present hankie around her fingers.

"Oh, Hilda, you have plenty of time ahead of you. I'm not going anywhere."

"I hope you're right."

Lily knew she wasn't. Hilda was deteriorating as surely as Magaly. She could hardly cross the room without getting out of breath and frequently had dizzy spells. They'd planned for a few years of fun and games after moving to the condo. It hadn't lasted long.

"How is Magaly?"

"I just came from her room. She's sleeping peacefully."

"Good. She suffers so much."

"I don't think for too much longer, Hilda. She's very weak."

"What will I do without her?"

"I'll be here for you, Hilda. I'm going to make the cocoa now."

Lily took two steaming cups into the living room.

"Look," Hilda said excitedly. "I found an Agatha Christie program."

Lily enjoyed these shows. She loved the Art Deco buildings, the old cars, the costumes, and the beautiful shots of lush English countryside. The plots were pretty good, too.

Hilda didn't make it through to the end, as Lily had predicted, so she recorded the show. She could put it on for her tomorrow afternoon. When the credits started to roll, Lily crept out to Magaly's room.

"Magaly, wake up." She shook her a little. "Just one pill this time."

She'd changed her mind about two pills after two hours. She'd only been gone for one hour, but a steady stream might work best. Magaly roused enough to swallow a pill before sinking back into sleep.

Lily went back to wake Hilda and help her to bed.

"Oh, Lily, it's so late. I worry about you going back alone in the dark."

"I think I'll sleep on the sofa tonight, Hilda."

"Oh, I'm so glad. I worry about you."

Lily worried about the effect it would have on Hilda if she discovered Magaly dead. She fell asleep and didn't wake up for a couple of hours. She went to Magaly. She couldn't wake her. Her breath seemed intermittent and shallow. Could this be it? It was a full hour before Magaly's breathing stopped altogether. Lily kissed her forehead for the last time and drew the sheet over her head.

Lily called hospice at six, and a nurse arrived within the hour.

"What time did it happen?"

"I'm not sure. I found her an hour ago. I stayed late last night, so slept on the sofa rather than go home in the dark. Magaly seemed worse than usual, too."

"In what way?"

"A lot of coughing, hard to catch her breath, weaker. I suppose it was inevitable. I'd better go and tell Hilda."

"Tell me what?" Hilda looked at the nurse, then at Lily, and burst into tears. She was in such a state the nurse took her pulse and called an ambulance. "Her heart rate is much too high."

Lily hugged Hilda, tears pouring down her own face. The ambulance came and took Hilda to the hospital.

Another came to take Magaly to the morgue.

"Were any arrangements in place?" asked the nurse.

"Yes, I helped Magaly with it a few months ago. Hilda, too, actually. I'd better call their attorney. I'll leave him to call their sons. None of them have taken care of their mothers."

"So often the case, I'm afraid," the nurse said. "I'd better be going now."

"I'm going to lock up and go home to shower and change. Then I'll go to be with Hilda."

"I'm so sorry. Were you close?"

"Very. I've been their only caregiver since Magaly became ill.

When Lily got to the hospital and asked for Hilda, she was asked to wait. A solemn young doctor came and escorted her to a private room. She knew Hilda was living on borrowed time. Was he going to tell her that? No, he told her that Hilda had passed away in the ambulance and the paramedics had been unable to revive her.

Lily managed to hold herself together enough to call the attorney again. She drove home and wandered around, not knowing what to do with herself. She felt Magaly's pills in her pocket. She swallowed two and went to bed.

25

Magaly and Hilda were cremated and their urns buried next to each other in the cemetery of a small Anglican church. Their sons did not attend. Lily received threatening phone calls from a couple of them when they discovered that Lily had inherited everything—small nest eggs and life insurance policies, plus the condo and its contents. She referred them to the attorney.

She was anxious to find Andrew but needed to get herself on an even keel first. She had to figure out how to get her money out of Canada. She would have the proceeds of the sale of her house, too. Perhaps she would leave one bank account open. But could she do that if she didn't have an address in Canada? So many things to take care of.

She must work on her novel, too. Sadness, trauma, write though it all, it kept her smooth. She'd written all kinds of scenes, but they needed rearranging. The love scene should come much later, but she'd needed to spit it out. She'd write an outline next, a story arc as Cecil used to call it. And in some way, she'd find her own new arc.

Cecil had suggested a couple of publishers who might accept her book. If it worked out, at least the creep had been good for something.

It took Lily four months before she finished her novel. To her surprise, one of the small publishers accepted it. It would be launched the following year. She could do all the required editing online, so no problem with a move. Having her novel accepted raised her spirits. It was an accomplishment. She'd used a pen name, Ivy Wallace, and there'd be a photo with glasses and yet another wig. She plucked up the courage to tell Wendy about the book and ask her if she could use her address for her bank account. She could just leave the royalties—if any—in Canada for the time being. She'd leave a small cushion, too. Things can change in seconds.

Should she risk hiding cash in her furniture shipment? She'd never paid American taxes whilst in Canada. Those sharks at the IRS wanted to fleece you any way they could. She'd figure it out. She always did. If she could get checks, and find someone in the U.S. to cash them for a fee? Maybe that would be the way to go. Or perhaps she could pay for a house with a Canadian direct deposit. She still knew some people who could help her evade detection. And she still had a fat account in the U.S.

She made some tea, and sat back in Hilda's armchair and thought about her protagonist.

Laura wanted a good life in a normal place, doing normal things. She wasn't afraid to admit it. That meant a good job, a good husband, and a nice home in a nice place. As a teenager, she used to go to the local drugstore and look through fancy magazines until she'd gathered up a dream, a dream she'd held onto: a white house with a tall fence and big old trees. Lots of green. Dream-trees that were a vague impression of the kind she'd seen in those magazines, hemming wonderful, perfect gardens that encircled wonderful, perfect houses. Yes, she wanted all of that, and babies, too. And she wanted to share those things with Gary. If she wished hard enough, dreamed enough, it would happen. She knew it would.

That was every woman's wish, wasn't it? It sounded too much like the beginning of her own journal, though. Someone might recognize it. No, no one knew of her dreams and aspirations. Except whoever might have read that journal. About four people, none of whom would dream of reading a romance novel. And this book would be unlikely to cross the border. Perhaps almost no one would read it.

Well, she'd had her day in the sun, her dream house and garden. And she blew it. She'd put all that behind her. Enough.

Would she write another story? Didn't she always?

1. Do you think the combination of Hilda and Magaly's influence changed Lily? Was one more influential than the other?

2. How did Lily affect Hilda and Magaly?

3. Why was Lily so keen on sightseeing in Toronto?

4. Lily came to regret her past violence. Do you think this regret was because she was caught or was it genuine?

5. Why did meeting Toby Elantro shake Lily so badly. Was it just because he might recognize her, or was there more to it?

6. Does Lily just happen to encounter criminal elements in these stories, or is she hypervigilant?

7. Lily promised herself she would not kill again. Did she break her promise for a good reason? Has she reformed?

8. What do you think of her choice to write romance novels?

9. Was Peter purely evil, or was he a victim, too?

10. Why do you think Lily really waited so long to go to find her son after the old ladies died?

Author Bio

D. A. Spruzen grew up near London, U.K., graduated from the London College of Dance and Drama Education, and earned an MFA in Creative Writing from the Queens University of Charlotte. She teaches creative writing in Northern Virginia when not seeking her own muse. She is the author of *The Flower Ladies Trilogy* and the *Sleuthing with Mortals* series. Other publications include a historical novel, The Blitz Business, and a poetry collection, *Long in the Tooth*. Her poems and short stories have appeared in many online and print publications. She resides in Northern Virginia and Southern Maryland. Her faithful companion, a Cavalier King Charles Spaniel named Sam, is always by her side, whether she's writing, painting, gardening, or reading yet another British mystery.

**Discover more at
4HorsemenPublications.com**

10% off using HORSEMEN10